CW00494163

North Star

Short Stories and Poems
by Female Northern Irish Writers

Women Aloud NI

Vision

"A community of female Northern Irish writers who work together to overcome challenges associated with gender, profession and place."

Mission

"To elevate the voices of female writers who live in Northern Ireland or who are from Northern Ireland."

North Star Editorial Team

Managing Editor
Kerry Buchanan

Editors
Lesley Walsh
Shelley Tracey
Orla McAlinden

Proofreader
Clare McWilliams

Project Manager
Angeline King

Contents

County Fermanagh

County Tyrone

Foreword

In January 2016, I joined a writing phenomenon called Women Aloud NI.

Jane Talbot, author of *The Faerie Thorn and Other Stories*, had managed to bring together a multitude of female writing talent, orchestrating gatherings across the province and in Dublin within weeks. In no time, Women Aloud NI was a bright star on the writing scene, known across the whole of the UK and Ireland, and further afield.

Today, Women Aloud is a large organisation with over 165 members. Among us are experienced writers, some of whom have been published by top international publishing houses and who have won awards at a national level, but we also have a diverse group of community-based writers, who write for fun.

In July 2019, I volunteered to be the new Chairperson of the community. I was impressed by how much energy people had dedicated to Women Aloud NI by organising events and maintaining a social media presence, and wondered how I might contribute. I saw my opportunity when Coronavirus sent the country into lockdown. I proposed a Women Aloud NI book.

The project would not have happened without the team behind it. Kerry Buchanan was at the helm with a spreadsheet that was poetic in its beauty and purpose, whilst Lesley Walsh, Orla McAlinden and Shelley Tracey rose to the challenge with enthusiasm and grace. Thanks goes to Ian Hooper and all at Leschenault Press, and I am also incredibly grateful to the writers, a constellation of bright individuals, who represent women in Northern Ireland like no group that has gone before them.

Angeline King
Chairperson,
Women Aloud NI,
2020.

County Antrim

We have five delightful pieces for you from County Antrim: We begin with a wistful poem by the talented **Shelley Tracey**, who also proofread many pieces for the anthology and edited the poetry for us. **Angeline King**, Chair of Women Aloud NI, and the woman behind this entire anthology, follows with a wonderful piece about the convoluted nature of family history.

An award-winning poem by **Angela Graham**, set in North Antrim, is next, before a change in mood and pace in the form of The Funnock Fairy Files, by **Vicky McFarland**, a whimsical piece written for children (and therefore enjoyable for adults, too!). Finally, we have a poem about Lisburn from the pen of **Yvonne Boyle**.

Belonging Time
Shelley Tracey

You come to this country from the heatlands, drift of dusty drygrass days in spring and summer, melting into copper sunsets, crickets ticking in the evening grass, keeping time with throbbing stars. In slow, unrolling motion, dung beetle up the hill. Glistening lizards stick to outer walls. The riverbeds are fossilised, no hint of flow.

Starting out your life in Lisburn, in rainblur, lossblur, for long, long whiles the pang of unbelonging, stumbled rhythms out of kilter, saying the wrong words out of time.

learning about belonging
            from the seasons
                    and the sky

High racks of clouds, the turtle doves' swift shadows on the glass, heading for the plane trees on the margins of the street. From your light-filled front room windows, the hillscape seems within your reach, presses the cathedral spire and rows of rooves and streets closer to your house.

Winter here is intimate, flames waving from the fireplace, naked winter branches, the gentleness of snowflakes drifting downwards, blending.

The soft approach of early spring. Snowdrops humbly cluster underneath the hedge. Clockfaces on forget-me-nots, always showing noon. Crocuses unfold in bolts of purple velvet. The simple miracle of bluebells, bluebells, bluebells all across the forest floor.

Summer flourishes. Pansies in their flouncy skirts. Crowding roses, each their own unfurling time. Hydrangeas lamp the garden. Gladioli, reaching high.

Autumn, unremarkable back home, the best of all the seasons here. A continuum of yellows, all the way from gold to brown. Such brave intensities just prior to decay, disintegration. Pages from the calendar unpeeling, letting go.

on the front doorstep
      waiting for the pulsing moon
           hours before the dark.

Shelley Tracey moved to Lisburn from Johannesburg over twenty years ago with three small children, one regular-sized husband, hundreds of books and a handful of published poems and stories. The children are now adults, the husband now comes with a dog, and there are many more books and published poems.

The Wedding Wisp
Angeline King

A dirl of rhyme filtered through the scullery as Cassie stacked the last wheaten farl onto the cooling-tray. Granny was singing about urchins, her hands twisting and plaiting a wisp of straw in her lap.

"Hae ye a wisp for the whole o Ballygally forbye Cairncastle?" teased Cassie, eyeing the overflowing basket by Granny's feet.

Granny gave a smile as taut as the straw she held in her hand. 'This bonnie wisp is goin naewhere."

"Da sez ye'll hae the devil upon us with your Hogmanay."

"If your da spent less time thinkin aboot the deil," said Granny, "he'd hae less work on his hands."

Cassie began clearing up the kitchen. All work had to be done before the first-footers crossed the threshold on New Year's Day, one of the superstitions Granny held onto despite her son-in-law's censure.

"It's brave an early to redd up the trimmings," said Cassie as she lifted the prickly holly from the chimney-brace.

"A clean hoose keeps bad omens oot!" said Granny.

"There'll be nae talk of bad omens in this hoose!" trumpeted Cassie, mimicking her father's unyielding voice.

Granny replied with a smile that doubled around her lips

5

like a plaited wisp of barley. It was a fearless expression, ready to deflect any man's chiding.

Cassie looked across the silver line of hawthorn outside the window. The moon shone white on a navy sky and the lights of the Maidens' lighthouses blinked yellow. She pictured her mother by the window, her paintbrush pointing to the horizon, her expression fearless.

***

Cassie clanged the brass bells to mark midnight and sipped back her whiskey. Granny leaned in close on the settle. "I met your granda at Hogmanay, ye ken?"

Cassie dropped her empty mug. Granda Scott's name was never mentioned.

"Och aye," said Granny. "The good Lord blow'd him through thon door. Hair as black as coal. I was leukin oot for weans beggin for bread and coal. But here, dear. The first-footer was Hamilton Scott frae Donaghadee. Lost in the fog after a danner up Sallagh."

Granny held up the short wisp of straw to reveal a heart shape where the loops of her creation intertwined. "I'd a wisp like this yin in my hand for the weans."

"Och, Granny," said Cassie, laughing. Hammy Scott was said to have died at sea, but Cassie had overheard a different tale the night of her mother's wake. As the sound of the fiddle echoed in the scullery, Granny Armstrong had whispered the truth to her sister, that Hamilton Scott had been a figment of Letitia Lynch's imagination. The pair of them had leaned over the open coffin and prayed for the soul of the dearly departed — Charlotte Scott, the bastard daughter.

"It's a cryin shame the weans dinnae still come first-footing roon here," said Cassie.

"Your da wouldnae stand for it. Beggars, he'd call them."

"Ma would hae said the same."

"Och, och anee," rhymed Granny. "Yer ma liked the oul ways when she was a wean. She aye gien your da his place as the heid o the hoose. And rightly so."

Cassie thought about her mother and her illness, the fatigue that died in the dim light. She would stay up half the night painting and then she would lie for days, not fit for lifting a hand. The Armstrongs said that Charlotte Scott was too much the lady, with her *painting* and *resting*.

Cassie missed her ma, but she'd never been drawn to the landscapes painted by her hand. She'd never been drawn to their colours, as dark as Haleve nicht.

"Granny," said Cassie. "Ye know there's mare a chance o' a draft blowin through thon door than a first-footer. Come on tae bed."

"Young yins! Where's the magic? I believed in magic. And leuk at me."

"Aye, leuk at ye, Granny," said Cassie, as she rattled the last of the slack from the bucket. "An oul widow wi nuthin but a sixteen year-oul tae warm them cowl feet. Let's get ye til yer bed."

***

Cassie's mind birled from the whisky. She tossed and turned half the night. At the stroke of five, a cold wind skimmed across her cheeks.

She slipped her hand into the icy air and switched on the gas lamp. Wind whistled through the chimney flue.

Cassie pulled back the heavy quilt and there was Granny. Nose tipped up. A gladsome smile. White hands gripping the heart-shaped wisp like a prayer.

Hands as cold as linen.

"Och, Granny," said Cassie.

There would be plenty of doing, once word spread to the Armstrong women that Letitia Scott had died, but even they knew better than to speak ill of the dead. There would be no more whispers about how or why Letitia Scott had bought her own house, or talk of a husband who had never been seen.

The first-footers would be dark, after all. Dark and in mourning. Maybe that's what Granny had planned. There would be wisps for all the mourners, and a house clean enough to accept their call.

But the first-footer had already been. He had snatched the last breath from Granny, then sped hastily on.

Cassie lifted the floorboard below her bed. There was something she needed to see before her father awoke and took over.

There was no marriage certificate for Letitia, but there was a birth certificate from Donaghadee First Presbyterian Church. Charlotte Lynch was the name of the child.

Cassie held the paper to her chest. Her mother was a Lynch and not a Hamilton.

There was also a solicitor's letter about the deeds of the house; it was dated 1881, the year before Charlotte was married. The name on it was Letitia Lynch.

Letitia Lynch had bequeathed the house to Cassie in her will, but no Armstrong would have the satisfaction of knowing the truth about Granny. Cassie would nail the floorboard down.

***

"There are Scotts on my maternal side."

Katie typed the words into Messenger after reading Simon Scott's blog. It was an easy distraction from the painting she could not finish. And after fruitless years of trying to trace the Scott side of her family, she had taken a notion that there might be a connection with Hamilton Scott, a once-celebrated portrait artist from Donaghadee. Perhaps she needed that connection to sustain her ebbing confidence in an artistic calling that had ripped her away from the security of nine to five.

As she waited for a response, she plotted a story for each of Hamilton Scott's paintings. There was the young woman who looked over her naked shoulder, back towards a mirror. There was an elderly woman with a half-smile and wrinkles so real that the canvas appeared cracked. Could it have been the same woman in her later years?

One more painting caught Katie's eye. A young boy with fair hair flying in the wind. 'First-Footer' was its name.

Katie studied the vigorous movement, then stood up and walked to her own unfinished canvas of a solitary woman.

She had seen the woman walk by the house one morning. Mothers and children were rushing past the window through a diesel fog, but the solitary woman appeared elegant and slow. Her red lips shone under a black umbrella.

Katie had painted the stranger in strokes of navy blue and black. She had painted dark shadows on her face that contrasted with the red lips shining. And she had tried to conjure up a story for the pain in the woman's smile.

She lifted a brush and dipped it in ochre. Sweeping it across the canvas, she felt movement through the bristles. A fair boy leaping. A boy who hadn't heeded his mother's cries.

And a mother. A mother who drew a line of composure on her lips each morning in red. A mother whose presence was a stone memorial walking.

Katie painted until, exhausted and empty, she stood back,

frightened by her own imagination. She had raised her daughter alone and, through her own night terrors, had many times lived out the darkness of losing a child.

***

It was after midnight when the Messenger alert sounded. Simon Scott had replied.

"Fascinating that your family is from Cairncastle. There is a landscape in the family collection called 'Cairncastle Sky Falling.' The name on it is C Scott. I've attached a photograph of it."

Katie studied the painting, the dark, gnarled hawthorn branches, the glints of light on the navy sea. She understood how to add light to her painting.

She drove to the derelict homestead in Cairncastle in the morning. Weeds strangled the remaining stones of the house. She thought about her ancestor, Letitia Scott. No one knew how she had acquired money to purchase a house. Granny Cassie had left no will, so the children of the Armstrong brothers had all made their own futile claim to the land. The matter had never been settled.

Katie climbed to the peak of the brae behind the homestead, where hawthorn trees jutted from the ground. In the distance, the sea was grey, but two lights blinked from the Maidens' lighthouses. She had found the painting by C Scott.

***

Simon Scott had selected the Ulster Reform club, a Victorian Gentleman's Club in the centre of Belfast, as the meeting venue.

"Awfully kind of you to come!" he said, as he clasped Katie's hand.

They sat in a panelled drawing room, below a curved window that looked out upon Belfast city centre, like a discerning eye.

"You've been busy," he said, placing his glasses on the end of his nose. He sifted through the documents Katie had compiled.

"This is from the 1911 census," she explained. "My great, great grandmother, Letitia Scott, is 72. Her daughter, Charlotte Armstrong, died in 1910. Charlotte's husband and their four sons are listed here and this is fourteen-year-old Cassie Armstrong, my grandmother."

"And Charlotte's maiden name was Scott?"

"Yes."

Simon's eyes rose to the wooden panelling. "I've searched, and there is no Letitia in our family tree. Come and have a look at this painting."

Katie followed him to the fireplace. She looked up. There she was, the same young woman that Katie had seen in the blog. She was clutching something in her hand, reaching towards the door as the wind lifted her brown hair.

"Hamilton was also an engineer," said Simon. "Founder member of this club. The painting is called 'The Wedding Wisp' and the detail is a feat of engineering in itself. Look at the folds of the wisp."

"What is it?"

"An old custom," said Simon. "She's greeting the first-footer of the year." He held out some photocopies. "There are five paintings by C Scott in the collection, including the one of Cairncastle."

"Charlotte," whispered Katie.

"The paintings are incredibly dark. More impressionistic than Hamilton's. There are some receipts for them. They went

11

for a good price in 1881. Hamilton sold them."

Katie looked up at the woman in the painting. Letitia had left something behind that would outlast any painting, straw, or stone – her mark was a fearless expression that thrived like hawthorn on dewy grass.

Katie read the brass plate.

> *No urchins came with hair alight*
> *For dark locks shone that windy night:*
> *An untamed brush on linen skin,*
> *Of ochre oils and knotted rings.*

Angeline King is the author of novels, *Snugville Street* (2015) and *A Belfast Tale* (2016), the history book, *Irish Dancing: The Festival story* (2018); a museum exhibition for MEA Council (2018) and an illustrated children's book called *Children of Latharna* (2017). Her latest novel, *Dusty Bluebells* is out in 2020.

The Scottish Referendum
Angela Graham

A View from Carraig Uisneach[*]

Two thousand years ago,
Deirdre of the Many Sorrows
unpinned her cloak
to pin it at her shoulder closer still,
as the shore of Ulster,
with every oar-stroke,
brought itself closer,
closer still.

Her lover, at this gesture,
shuddered
– once out of Scotland,
their lives were fastened
to the fragile promise
of a hungry king.
On this rock, facing Rathlin,
Great Conor's men
waited for her, uneasily.
Extremes – even of beauty –
unbalance everything.
This sea is still sometimes too blue.
A mineral cobalt, gleaming enamel

penned in the compartments of a brooch,
it fills the channels bounded by the lines of shores
and hugs the blunt bronze bosses of the islands;
a cold, fluid metal; a road that shivers
between Uladh and Alba.

The promise of a king
cannot bind closer or undo
this cloisonné of straits and headlands.
Mist clears to reveal, sun strikes into view
the flanks of Scottish sea-loughs
jig-sawing towards us.

Causeways – from Antrim, from Argyll – intend,
striving to meet.
These cliffs and coastlines were a kingdom once,
bright Dal Riada;
its highways water;
harbours, the gates and outskirts of its towns.

But what realm's fixed forever?
Allegiances pleat, one on the other,
like dogged breakers brokering a bay.

As the folds of a cloak are slackened off or gathered
by the placement of a pin,
at this north-eastern shoulder
sometimes we pull the Irish, sometimes the Scots,
a little closer in
and we acknowledge,
with Islay, Jura, Arran and Kintyre,
our never-changing governance:
winds off the Atlantic, the astringent rains.

*Carraig Uisneach is a rock jutting out from Ballycastle Beach, County Antrim. From ancient times it was a point of arrival from, and departure for, Scotland. Deirdre of the Sorrows risked returning to it from safe haven in Scotland with the three Sons of Uisneach, her lover, Naoise and his brothers, **Uladh** and **Alba**: Gaelic names for Ulster and Scotland

The H'mm Foundation, to mark the Scottish Referendum on Independence, 2014, commissioned four poets, one from each of the constituent parts of the U.K., to write for performance. This was the Northern Irish perspective. The other poets were Gillian Clarke (National Poet of Wales, 2008 -2016); Professor Jasmine Donahaye, and Christine De Luca (Edinburgh Makar: poet laureate for the City of Edinburgh, 2014 – 2017).

Angela Graham's poetry has appeared in *The North, The Interpreter's House* and elsewhere. Seren Books publishes her short story collection, *A City Burning* in September 2020. Her novel on the politics of language in N. Ireland and book of prose and poetry on Place and Displacement there are supported by Arts Council NI SIAP Awards. Follow her at Twitter @AngelaGraham8, and www.angelagraham.org.

The Funnock Fairy Files
Vicky McFarland

April 10th

OK, let's just get this out in the open. Fairies exist. Fact. And not just fairies; trolls, leprechauns, mermaids, elves — pretty much every magical creature you've ever heard stories about, they're real. I know you probably think that's nonsense, and that I'm making these stories up to entertain you, but I promise, I could not make this stuff up. I don't have enough imagination. These are things that actually happened to me (and my sister Keeley) when we moved to The Funnock (aka Carnfunnock Country Park) in County Antrim.

Funnock File 1: A Fairy Festation

We first knew we had a problem when three Easter Weekend caravans decided to scarper — and when I say scarper, I mean career out of the campsite at the full five miles an hour, toilet roll hanging from the windows, disposable barbeques left smoking in their wake. This would be OK, dare I say normal, except they did this on Good Friday morning, having only just arrived the night before, and they did *not* ask for their money back. It was odd. Not unheard of — quite a lot of people leave The Funnock when they get a look at the toilet block — but

16

three was extreme. And no demand for their money back? Suspicious.

I decided to investigate.

At the scene, I found a trail of mud, sticks and leaves. It could mean only one thing: we had a Fairy Festation.

What To Do When You Get A Fairy Festation

1. Cry, pull your hair, stamp your feet, scream (whatever makes you feel better)

2. Call the Fairy Refuser (not to be confused with a Fairy Excuser, which is a totally different thing, and only needed if your Fairy Festation goes feral)

So, after jumping up and down on the spot and stamping my feet for five minutes, I called the only Fairy Refuser I knew: Big Pete.

Big Pete was busy. It was Easter weekend, he had a list of jobs as long as his nose, and if he could get to us, he would try, but we were probably talking Tuesday at the earliest.

Tuesday would be too late.

If a Fairy Festation is allowed to fester for more than a day, it turns feral, and then you really are in trouble. So, I did what I had to do… I dealt with it myself.

Correction: He called his brilliant, smarter, younger sister to come and sort it out for him.

The first thing to do when you have a Fairy Festation is to identify the fairies. By that I mean the *type* of fairies. There are a lot of different types of fairies, and they all fester for different reasons and in different ways. I knew that this had to be Woodland Fairies, because they had arrived at the scene on woodland transportation (the leaves, sticks, mud, etc.), but there is a plethora of Woodland Fairies to choose from.

Most Common Woodland Fairies

1. Beav-airies: these fairies are busy beavers, always building something (festations happen when they have a big project and a need to steal a lot of equipment)

2. Tramp-airies: these fairies love to tramp mud and dirt all over the cleanest and tidiest places they can find (festations occur when there is a special event and too many get together, encouraging each other in their tramping)

3. Tittle-airies: these fairies like to gather to tittle-tatter about other fairies (a festation is harmless, but quite noisy)

4. Conk-airies; usually seen in autumn, these fairies love to throw conkers at unsuspecting humans (festations can be quite painful)

5. Prank-airies; the worst kind of fairy, they will do anything to make each other laugh (a festation means trouble – big trouble)

It didn't take me *(correction: Keeley and me)* long to ascertain that our Fairy Festation was made up of prank-airies.

We were going to have to act fast.

Picking up their trail was easy enough; we just had to follow the sound of outrage and tears. Campers had woken up to find breakfast materials decorating their windscreens, mud-stained knickers hanging from their wing mirrors, and one family had fairy-sized holes cut out of every item of clothing. It was getting bad.

The problem with fairies (and this goes for all types of fairies) is that they're super quick and hard to catch. To stop our festation of prank-airies from going feral, we had to call in the Big Nose: Snouser, our grumpy and fairy-weary Chocolate Labrador.

Officially, Snouser was in retirement. We had started training his replacement, The Colonel, but unfortunately he was proving tricky (he had oodles of enthusiasm, but no self-control, meaning that he often got over excited and peed everywhere), so Snouser would have to step up.

Only problem was, Snouser had taken the opportunity of retirement to indulge his love of biscuits, so now he was not only grumpy, but also quite fat and painfully slow.

Keeley coaxed him out of his basket by bribing him with his favourite chocolate treats, but it took at least twenty minutes to drag him the ten yards to the caravan pitches, by which time the fairies were long gone. This would have been okay if he had even a sniff of the old fire in him, but the minute he caught a whiff of fairy scent, he sat down in the middle of the road and flat refused to budge. I guess some dogs are as resistant to old tricks as they can be to new ones.

"Shall we try the Colonel?" Keeley asked.

Always eager, the Colonel bounded around the caravans, lapping up cheerios and sniffing muddy knickers, much to the horror of the campers (who had, quite frankly, had enough disruption for one Easter break).

We were just about to take him home, when he picked up a scent and went careering into the bushes. Ever hopeful, Keeley and I darted after him, leaving Snouser happily snoozing in the sun.

This is probably a good point for me to try to describe a fairy.

Describing a fairy can be difficult, because their magic has a strange effect on the human brain. After you've seen one, it's hard to keep hold of the memory; the image sort of lingers at the edge of your mind. As long as you don't look too hard at it, you'll remember, but if you pay it any kind of attention, it disappears in a puff of fairy dust.

Nevertheless, I'll do my best: they're small, about a foot high. They don't have wings but they do have…

No, it's gone. I can't remember. Just use your imagination.

We followed the Colonel through the brambles, getting scratches on our legs, and trying to avoid treading in dog poo. Keeley stepped in a massive pile and had a bit of a hissy fit, *(you would too, it stank! Why can't people just put their dog poo in the bins provided?)* which meant we almost lost the Colonel's trail. Luckily, he started barking and we found him jumping about and peeing in front of a tree. Halfway up was a squirrel. With a nut.

Back to square one. But not for long, because we heard a scream. It was coming from the maze.

Not good. The maze is Troll Territory.

The Colonel, Keeley and I arrived at the entrance to the maze to find a toddler with an ice cream on her head. Thankfully, the toddler wasn't upset, although her mum was.

"Angela! What did you do that for?"

"It was the fairies!"

"Don't lie."

"*I'm not lyyyy-ing!*"

It's fair to say, the toddler was quite upset by the time we left them to it.

We headed into the maze. If you think the worst thing a Fairy Festation can do is attack humans, you're wrong. Humans have a wonderful ability to tell themselves all sorts of stories to explain the unexplainable. Trolls, on the other hand, will accept the fairies at face value and protect themselves, usually by using violence, and nearly always with great pomp and ceremony.

In the middle of the maze, we found a troll army, complete with fox cavalry, a band of trash instruments and Ismareelda, the Troll Queen herself, in full battle armour – made of recycled food containers and bottles (FYI; trolls love rubbish; whenever you see a bin with all the contents strewn about, that's usually them).

They were singing their battle song, which goes a bit like this:

Come and fight us, we will win.
We are trolls, and we will win.
Win win win win, win win win.
Trolls in fights will always win!

As you might have gathered, trolls like to win. Along with the singing, which generally is out of time and accompanied by that horrendous screeching foxes do, they were banging their rubbish about and making a right old ruckus.

There was no sign of the fairies.

Or so we thought.

Suddenly, from out of the hedge to our left, a missile came flying. It passed over Keeley's head and landed slap-bang on Queen Ismareelda's nose. The singing stopped. The screeching died away. All the trolls held a collective breath.

Queen Ismareelda's eyes looked down at her nose, which scrunched up in disgust. The prank-airies had pond-bombed her! (A pond-bomb is a fistful of pond matter, wrapped up in a ball of moss, the gunkier the better). Slime, gunge, and something gooey that didn't belong anywhere near a face slowly dripped down her bulbous nose.

"*Get them!*" shouted Queen Ismareelda.

The assembled trolls (of which there were about fifty, including ten riding on foxes) charged at the hedge.

Unfortunately, trolls are thick in stature as well as in mind and even though they hurled themselves at that hedge with vigour, most of them simply got stuck. Those that did make it through to the other side found themselves attacked by yet more pond-bombs, which came from the left, the right and up above. Where fairies are quick, trolls are cumbersome. By the time the army had wriggled its way through the hedge, the fairies had clambered over them and taken Queen Ismereelda's throne.

Luckily, they were so distracted by the fight that they didn't see us hiding behind the throne. As the fairies (of which we only counted five) laughed and pointed and stuck their tongues out at the trolls, Keeley and I were able to grab two.

Nothing ruins a Prank-airy's fun like being dangled upside down by their feet. Keeley had one, I had the other. The three remaining Prank-airies stamped up and down, complaining about the unfairness of the situation and demanding that we should put their friends down right now, or there would be trouble.

The Colonel popped his head up and licked his lips.

That shut the fairies up.

Now, I should mention that despite the fact that fairies can be very annoying, and that when a Festation breaks out, you have to take action before it gets out of hand, we do respect and love our fairies in The Funnock.

So, we would never, ever let the Colonel eat one. We just let the fairies think it might be a possibility.

I took the opportunity to remind the fairies of our agreement:

Humans and fairies of the Funnock live
together in harmony and with respect.

They were disappointed that their fun was over, but we gave them each a small Easter egg and they went away happy. That night, we took the hoses up to the maze and gave the trolls a sprinkler party.

This went some way towards making them feel better as well as towards cleaning away the pond muck.

That was the end of the Fairy Festation.

File Closed

Vicky McFarland is a children's storyteller and writer. Originally from England, Vicky has made her home in County Antrim with her husband and two children. Her favourite place to walk is Carnfunnock Country Park, which has inspired this little tale.

Castle Street, Lisburn
Yvonne Boyle

Our parents moved from Fairview House to Castle Street.
Our dad's new shop a walk away in Market Square.

A great address - that's what I thought when growing up
in Lisburn, number 36 in Castle Street.

Two shops below and us two floors above.
High ceilings, window views
and evening light down Castle Street.

We played in the Castle Gardens park
until it was time for tea, a few doors down in Castle Street.

We walked to school, a sister's hand
at traffic lights, two blocks away from Castle Street.

My mother's ancestor lived there
and Granda met my Grandma
at a dance in Market Square near Castle Street.

The night the bomb went off. No-one was hurt,
although my Mum was blown up the hall.
No windows left in Castle Street.

We moved when I was seventeen, I wondered why,
to Belsize Road, just not the same as Castle Street.

I've lived in many towns and I have learnt
that architecture can be kind and buildings
can help to raise a child in Castle Street.

It's the historic quarter now. Ground floor,
my sister's gallery. And children play again
on the arcade swing in Castle Street.

Yvonne Boyle has had a range of poems published, in 'Cobalt Blue',
Dunfanaghy Writers' Circle (2016); the Bangor Literary Journal; Com-
munity Arts Partnership's Poetry in Motion Anthology (2017/18). She
works as a sessional Community Arts Partnership Artist-Facilitator and
is a NI Arts Council (SIAP) Awardee (2018/19) who is working on her
first pamphlet.

County Armagh

*We bring you an orchard of delights from fruitful County Armagh. The first piece is a moving story, woven by **Céline Holmes**, followed by a romp through one family's past, written by **Orla McAlinden**, who also proofread much of the anthology.*

*Next, we have **Byddi Lee**, who brings us a sad tale of the terrible railway disaster that occurred in Armagh in 1889, followed by an amusing tale of Portadown as you've never seen it before from **Lorna Flanagan**. Finally, **Adeline Henry**'s Glorious and Grand brings a gentle, pastoral ending to this chapter.*

In Memoriam
Céline Holmes

I follow the daffodils. I saw the first one yesterday, spray-painted at the bottom of a gable, around the corner from my house. This morning, there was another. They were my son's favourite flowers. He said they reminded him of his mother. I don't know why; he was too young to remember her. He used to grow them in our back garden each spring, a symbol of hope and rebirth. Now, my back garden's a mess of overgrown bushes and dead plants.

There are ten daffodils, one for each year he's been gone, and they lead me past the garage, towards the station. The last one's under a bridge.

The bridge.

A young man is spray-painting on a wall. I watch for a while before I recognize him. His hair's longer and dirtier, but it's Danny, my son's best friend. Shamefully, I realize I'd forgotten he even existed. Yet they were inseparable from an early age.

'It's you,' I say, without saying hello. I stopped greeting people a long time ago, as if it would ease my grief.

He smiles shyly.

'The flowers on his grave.' I stopped visiting the cemetery after the first anniversary of his death, the weight of my double loss too heavy to carry. But I was told there are always fresh flowers on Bobby's and his mum's graves. Until today, I'd had no idea who'd been putting them there.

He nods quietly. 'I was hoping you'd come.'

I follow his gaze and see a giant portrait of my son spray-painted on the wall, his face framed by daffodils. *Forever Young* is written below, covering an old graffiti that said: *Religion is a plague,* and its cutting retort: *So is your Ma.*

I may be a bit biased, but I prefer the new one.

'Ten years ago today, they found him here, stabbed to death,' I say.

'I know. I was there.'

I look at him. They had found my son alone, in a pool of blood.

'He died because of me.'

I frown. The police arrested the culprit, years ago. Also released him from prison years ago. 'You didn't stab him.'

'He was my…' He bites his lip. 'We were…'

Our gaze meets. My eyes widen.

'I had no idea.'

It makes sense. Why Bobby never brought a girl home. I thought that, dying at eighteen, he'd never known love.

'We'd taken the last train from Belfast that night, and we were walking home, holding hands,' he says after a while. 'A group of boys started mocking us. I fought back, they attacked us. One of them had a knife.' Tears streak his face. 'Bobby stepped in to protect me…'

I hug Danny. 'He saved you,' I whisper, a lump in my throat.

***

30

The following week, Danny and I buy sandwiches from Tesco and go to Edenvilla Park for a walk. There's a secret garden with wooden sculptures and a maze that I didn't even know existed. I can't remember the last time I went for a wee dander in Portadown. I only go out for food, now. When Bobby was still alive, I used to take the dog out every day. After my son was killed, I would let the dog out in the back garden, so I wouldn't have to meet people's gaze, their eyes full of fake pity.

Then the dog died.

We sit on a bench. The air's still cold, but it's a bright and sunny day.

'We didn't know.'

'Huh?'

'That we were gay. It just happened one day. It felt normal.'

'I wish I'd known.'

'Bobby was scared of how you'd take the news.'

'I wouldn't have let you take the train late at night.'

Danny lowers his head. The sad thing is, he's probably right. Back then, I would have been furious and I'd have ordered Bobby never to see Danny again. But now that I know the pain of loss, the fact that my son was gay seems so trivial, so unimportant.

'We can't change the past,' I say, grabbing the remnants of our improvised picnic. I toss the rubbish in a nearby bin and gesture towards the car park.

'Shall I give you a lift home?'

Danny looks embarrassed. 'Sure,' he says hesitantly before picking up his huge backpack.

'Where's home?' I know his parents left Portadown a few years back.

Danny shrugs. 'Anywhere.'

I notice the sleeping bag hanging from the rucksack. 'Don't tell me you sleep rough?'

He sighs. 'My parents kicked me out when I came out. I don't make a lot of money from my paintings.'

I'm saddened, but not surprised. His father was an elder at the church I stopped going to. I look at the daffodils in the flowerbeds, and I think of Bobby. I know what he would have wanted me to do.

'My house is too big for me.'

He gives me a quizzical look.

'You no longer have a father, and I lost my son. But we can fix that.'

Danny slings his bag over his shoulder and follows me home.

Céline Holmes lives in Lurgan but is from Normandy, France. She's been working on a family saga and is currently editing the first novel while writing up the second. Earlier this year, she had a poem published in a writing magazine for the first time.

The Big Fat Chernadrine
Orla McAlinden

'Get up and get on ye, ye lazy wee hallions!' I burst through the door of my sons' bedroom and find them, anti-socially distanced, in front of their laptops, ploughing through their Corona-virus-mandated, remote-learning secondary school lessons.

'Get up and get on ye,' I roar at Number One son, 'and don't be sitting there like a big, fat chernadrine.'

By the time I am finished raising Number One son, he's going to be eminently qualified for a job as hostage negotiator, or psychotherapist. He is completely inured to my eccentricities.

'What's going on, mum? Is it some Facebook thing?'

'Yeah, you're such a Boomer,' chortles Number Two son, who is destined for a less diplomatic career.

'I'm twenty years too young to be a Boomer, you cheeky wee blirt, I just want to know if you know that *Get up and get on ye* used to mean *Get dressed*.'

In his calmest, most soothing voice, Number One points out that they are, in fact, both fully dressed. I put my head in my hands.

'No, no, no. The only acceptable response to the phrase is "I *am* on me!" If I put this in my novel, will anyone know what

I mean?'

'Mum, I don't think we're really your target audience,' says Number One.

'Maybe some of the other Boomers will understand,' snorts Number Two, and I close the door on the sound of their laughter.

***

Since I penned my first work of fiction, after my father's death in 2012, I have come to realise the awful aching loss of the rich rural Ulster dialect that surrounded me in my youth. I am in my mid-forties, and these days I attend more funerals than weddings, most recently that of Ben Fearon of Kilmore and Portadown, a man who could have written the book on our vernacular. My first collection of short stories, *The Accidental Wife,* was dedicated to my parents, and to Ben and his wife, Nellie, "whose voices echo through these pages."

When I was young, I suspected Ben must be rich, because he owned a beautiful brown and cream leather edition of the Encyclopaedia Britannica, whose gold-embossed spines filled an entire bookcase in his book-crammed home. And it was to the borrowed C-volume of his encyclopaedia that I turned to research the mystery of the big fat chernadrine. I could, of course, just have asked him what it was, but that was beneath my ten-year-old dignity.

The mystery of the big, fat chernadrine had haunted my middle childhood. I knew it was a large and heavy beast, characterised by immense sloth and lack of drive. I knew it was a dreadful insult. *Get up ou' a that and don't be sittin' there, muggin' about like a big, fat chernadrine,* Ben would bellow when he needed help to move his half-crazed bullocks from field to poorly-fenced field. Sighing, I would peel myself reluctantly from the smoky, diesel-coaxed fire in the vast fireplace of the ruined farmhouse in the townland of Mulladry in Armagh, and head off into the persistent, sullen drizzle.

Take a gunk at thon wee cyarn on the news, sitting there like a big, fat chernadrine; he wouldn' work ta warm himself, grumbled my father, as he settled down in front of *Scene around Six* to listen to all the woes of the day.

I was consumed with curiosity about the chernadrine, and outraged by my ignorance. I knew an ocelot from an otter, a hawk from a handsaw. I could spell *palaeontologist* and use *recidivist* in a sentence without blinking. I could not bear to hear this elusive animal's name taken in vain all around me, without some idea of its appearance, its habitat and habits. I told Ben I needed his C-encyclopaedia to research a school project about St Catherine of Siena, and flicked eagerly to the page which should, but did not, explain the mysterious big fat chernadrine. Stubborn does not begin to describe me. I would not ask. I would use my prodigious genius to work it out for myself, no matter how long it took.

Instead, in time, I just stopped caring.

Many other terms have disappeared from rural Ulster's common parlance since those times. Some were quaint, even then. Naughty children attracted a range of colourful, abusive epithets such as *wee blirt* or *wee cyarn*; foolish ones were *wee stumers*. An overtired, whingeing youngster was a *pishmire*. A petulant or spoiled brat was a *wee nyark*.

When I was young, any boastful or self-aggrandising tale was immediately countered with *Aye right, and your bum's beef, I suppose*. A naïve person had *just floated down the Bann in a bubble*. If your plans were ambitious or outlandish, you needed to have a *tither of wit,* or to *catch yerself on*. We weren't careless, we were *throughother*. We didn't tell each other to eff off, we called down *hell's curse on ye*. Today's dull *I've got a bad cough* was the vividly onomatopoeic *I was up all night, blaugherin' and hoggerin'*.

To describe childish antics, we called on a voluminous vocabulary: *acting the lig, acting the maggot, jacking about (like a jackass), behaving like a latchiko* (your guess is as good as mine). And the incredibly withering *yer head's a marley*.

In time, we children learned to swear like troopers, as farmers and neighbours gradually ceased to censor themselves in our presence. We started to acquire responsibilities and tasks and freedoms of our own. We roamed the country lanes and fields of Mulladry, Derryhale, Drumnahunshin, and Bottlehill. We ate blackberries and wild strawberries in abundance, and sniffed tiny wild roses in the bedraggled hedges. We brought home the mini mushrooms that sprang up overnight. We tortured Mrs Cochrane with our 'unexpected' appearance at mealtimes and snack times, and leaned over the counter at old Mrs Chapman's post office to buy paper bags of sweets, then disappeared into the farmhouse to drink her cows' fresh unpasteurised milk. Decades later, I stole one of Granny Chapman's phrases and put it in a book. *The shap-bought milk is fit for nathin. It doesn't even colour the tay.*

We *helped make* hay. We dragged those heavy, sweet-smelling bales into groups for later collection, the coarse twine biting through our gloves, reddening and coarsening our palms. We sat on top of rickety trailers, piled fifteen feet high with hay, on the short trip back to the farmyard. Those were joyous journeys that, today, would have any right-minded mother applying for sole custody of her children. These memories and emotions surface time and again in my writing, in my books *The Accidental Wife* and *Full of Grace*.

In time, by osmosis, we learned the deep-rooted ancestral animosities of the townland. We knew whose grandfather had insulted whose uncle at a market-day, decades past; who had 'poached' a field from the rightful buyer, by sending a dummy bidder to the auction.

Another transgressor had 'blown in' to the area and built a large imposing house (positively modest by today's standards), marring the pastoral view of a hereditary-dweller on the country road. 'Building his bloody mansion, like Lord Don' know who!' raged the offended bungalow-dweller. The interloper was known, ever after, behind his back, as Lord Donoghue.

It is perfectly possible that his son is now called 'Young Donoghue', and I wonder how many people would remember why.

To block out the view of Lord Donoghue's 'mansion' (three fields away), the aggrieved man surrounded *his own small* residence with a wall of Leylandii trees, condemning his home to dreary darkness. 'Men do this kind of thing,' my mother explained, with a sigh, when I related the story to her.

'Yer man is a complete gulpin,' my father added succinctly. I immediately added *gulpin* to the list of desperately uncouth *country-munchie* words that I would never utter again. For I had a plan. I was going to escape these guttural, coarse dialects and I was moving to Dublin at the earliest opportunity. I would strip this embarrassing layer of the vocal-clabber of Armagh from my pelt, and emerge anew from my cocoon: vibrant, urban, sophisticated, and, if at all possible, Californian. I would not teach my children archaic and humble expressions such as *get up and get on ye*, or *houl' yer horses*. I would listen to Tom Waits, not Big Tom. I would read Flannery O'Connor, not John O'Connor. No matter how long it took, or how hard the struggle, I would, eventually, be COOL!

Fourteen years old, and several years into my self-imposed exile from my native argot, I helped clear out the semi-derelict farmhouse at Mulladry. To our great excitement, Benedict Jr. was marrying, and taking formal charge of the farm.

In years past, my father had occasionally hoisted us children on his shoulders, allowing us to creep up the farmhouse staircase, which had been destroyed by fire decades ago. We picked our way across splintering, fire-damaged boards and rotten joists, roaming the bedrooms untouched since the death of old Barney Fearon. John F. Kennedy and Pope John XXIII glared down at us as we poked at the ancient crumbling bed-hangings and pulled long strips of curling distemper from the walls. Gaudy statues of the Virgin Mary and the Child of Prague stood still on dressing tables. Chamber-pots nestled under the beds.

Now, all was change. The staircase must be replaced, the bedrooms gutted and prepared to receive the new bride. The parlour and the scullery must be emptied and somehow converted to a modern living-room and kitchen. Grunting, Ben rolled a huge oak dash-churn from the scullery into the old kitchen. 'What'll I do wi' thon?' he pondered. 'I sometimes see eejits a' town-people plantin' flowers in them oul churns. I say, I say, John, would it be worth money?'

I plunged the massive dash up and down through the tight-fitting hole in the lid. Generations of Fearon women had dashed thousands of gallons of cream in that churn until the protein and fats caught together to produce golden farmhouse butter. I saw my father and Ben smirk as my frail arms ached and trembled after a half-dozen strokes.

'Oh, you wouldn't be so generous spreading your butter if you had to make it the old way,' they laughed, 'instead of buying it from Golden Cow!'

They reminisced about the bright yellow butter of their childhood, the sharp, tangy buttermilk, about the smuggling of butter across fields and ditches in days of wartime rationing.

'Oh, cleanin' thon churn was a bitter task too, crawlin' damn-near inside the oul' drum, scrubbing with a hard deck-brush, sluicing wi' boiling water carried from the scullery beyond to the dairy. Then wedging it in the hearth; a-steaming beside the fire. I say, I say John, d'you mind the awful, choking smell of the big, wet churn a-dryin?'

Dedicated to my mother, Barbara McAlinden, safely cocooned. And to the memories of John McAlinden and Ben and Nellie Fearon.

Orla McAlinden is an award-winning author from Co Armagh, living in Kildare. Her books *The Accidental Wife* and *Full of Grace* depict seventy years in a rural Ulster community and *The Flight of the Wren* is a novel exploring the survival, through crime, of women in the Irish Famine period.

Searching the Wreckage
Byddi Lee

Armagh 1889

Mangled metal creaks and groans as rescuers climb over the carcass of the carriages, shouting through windows, searching, hoping, many weeping as they work. Frantic women pass crying children through carriage windows into the arms of strangers. Men ferry the wounded down the sloping embankment to scurrying helpers. Some people wander listless and dull-eyed around the field of wreckage and debris spilling down the hillside. The clang of iron on iron rings through the orchestra of cries and groans, a percussion of pain in a symphony of chaos.

'Help me here,' one man calls, close enough to jolt Lottie from her stunned scanning of the carnage. She turns to see a man, his face a mask of blood, dragging an unconscious woman. The loll of the head and the mass of dark hair loose across the woman's face is almost unseemly – too intimate a dishevelment for strangers to witness. Stretcher-bearers race to the man.

Where is George?

Lottie's hands twist in her apron. She never wears it outside of work, but she'd not had time to remove it when she heard the calls ring through the city to come help. She applies her gaze with more intention this time, straining to focus on faces before wounds, to look past the cream bone protruding through red-raw skin and frayed cloth below a knee, to see the person screaming above it. She should know these people. Everyone knows everyone in Armagh, but here, now, she doesn't recognize anyone, wracked as they are in their agonies.

If George is hurt, or worse…

She drags her mind from that idea. Find him first, no point in useless speculation.

She sets off up the embankment until she reaches a young girl, no older than eight, lying on her back. Her crisp white dress bears a dark smudge of dirt across the chest. Lottie stares, wondering how, in all this clatter and shouting, can the girl sleep? Then she notices that the child's ice-blue eyes gaze, unblinking at the sky. Lottie's heart chills as she picks out the dark red trickle travelling from the child's ear, down her neck and disappearing into the dark shiny wad of hair splayed around her shoulders. The girl is dead. The shattering knowledge freezes Lottie's limbs.

Nearby, two toddlers pick buttercups. One drops yellow petals on the grass. The other yawns and rubs her eyes. She looks at Lottie with a tear-stained face, her lower lip wobbles before she points to the dead child, saying, 'Nory, Nory.' The other toddler, older by a year or so perhaps, totters over and grabs the other by the hand. The two wander back and sit by the dead girl.

Sorrow bubbles up, piercing the shock that has numbed Lottie until this point. Her stomach glides up, then down again. With legs like lead weights, she grapples for control, forcing herself to take a step up the bank towards the shattered remains of the train.

Find him.

Above her, a woman's wail grips the air. It reverberates in the pores of Lottie's skin. She looks up and sees her friend, Sarah, fall to her knees beside a bundle of bloody cloth and rags. The wail terminates in a split-second gasp of relative silence before yells for help and screams of agony fill in again. Sarah buries her face in her hands. Lottie reaches her friend and wipes the wet heat from her own eyes before seeing that the bundle of rags is the torso of Sarah's husband, John. Only mangled flesh remains where his legs should be.

Lottie breathes in ragged puffs and drops to her knees. She should stay with Sarah, forget about looking for George.

He is either alive…

Lottie rubs her bruised ribs.

…Or he isn't.

Sarah's grief is contagious. Sucking in breaths, Lottie struggles to compose herself, but her eyes fill and overflow as she clings to her friend, grateful for the warmth from Sarah's body against her chest.

Above them, along the tracks, the engine lies upside down with its wheels in the air – a ludicrous pose. Another carriage lies in splinters strewn down the bank interspersed with bodies. Two more damaged carriages sit off the track, but upright.

Lottie tries to remember what their seat numbers had been. She'd given both tickets to George telling him to go on without her. Had she not had such fresh bruising on her lower legs, she might have accompanied him to the seaside. But what was the point, she'd asked him, when she couldn't take off her shoes and walk on the sand with him?

He'd been sheepish, hungover too. A day by the sea would clear his head. He'd come home a changed man, starting today, he'd promised. The wheel of their marriage would turn, as usual, past this rickety-click and onto the smooth – till the next round.

A man in dirty white britches, his Sunday best ruined for all time, stumbles down the slope towards them. Lottie recognizes him but can't place him.

'Are there many –' she says.

The man's voice is fast and shaky as he rattles his report, 'No survivors in the last carriage. So many injured. Oh, God, so many.' He lurches on past her.

The last carriage, third class. The only tickets Lottie and George could afford. She struggles to her feet and leaves Sarah keening and rocking by her husband. Sarah doesn't look up.

The walk up the hill toward the rubble of the last carriage drags at Lottie as if she is wading up to her knees into the sea in her dress and full petticoats.

'Don't come up here, Missus.' A young man with tear tracks on his grimy face blocks her way.

'Please, I need–' But Lottie doesn't know what she needs, or wants.

She pictures George when he's not possessed with the demon drink, his face alight with the smile of a million suns, warming her heart and setting her soul aflame.

In sickness and in health...

Lottie presses her thumb into the bruise on her ribs, the pain replacing the memory of his curved lips and dimpled cheeks with fury and fists.

...Until death do us part.

It's as if right here, right now, she alone has the choice. If she chooses a life without the beatings, it will be as simple as blowing out a candle. She can hear the soft 'phuff' as the flame extinguishes and she sees herself clad in black, then grey, then eventually in delicate pink.

Fear wicks the moisture from her mouth and stampedes her heartbeat.

'I have to find him,' Lottie's voice says a beat before she really decides.

'Who?' the young man asks.

'George Turner.'

'I know George.'

'You do?'

'Aye, I'm Tom. His apprentice.'

'Yes, yes, of course, you are. Sorry, I didn't–'

'That's okay, Mrs Turner,' the lad says and smiles, a ray of sun in a stormy sky. 'I haven't seen him. 'Do you know what type of ticket he had?'

Lottie tries to speak, but it only comes out as a croak.

Tom ducks to catch the sound as if his ear could scoop it up as it drops from her lips.

Lottie swallows, her throat too brittle, too dry. Her hand floats up. She points at the ruins of the last carriage.

'I'll take you down to wait below. We're clearing the bod– the people out of there now.' His hand is firm on her shoulder.

Lottie allows him to guide her back down the slope. They pass Sarah, who is still on her knees, crouched over her husband, clasping his hand, sniffing quick gusts of air in and shuddering breaths out. Tremors travel the length of Sarah's body to where her knees connect with the sod. A cleric kneels with her, bent crow-like, his eyes closed and Lottie feels a hot gust of anger towards his ineffectiveness but presses on. Hope has no place here.

The dead girl and the toddlers are gone, but Lottie sees the flattened grass. A scrap of white material flutters on a bramble by a pile of crushed buttercups.

The meadow has become a staging area with the wounded treated on site. Dark red soaks the clothes of so many, Lottie can barely tell the injured from those administering to them. She recognizes many of the injured. Friends, relatives, neighbours. She cannot, dare not, offer them comfort. Her mind flees their collective pain. Guilt sizzles beneath her horror at their injuries and her sorrow for their suffering. Those who can, turn from her, while others too far-gone with pain and shock stare in her direction with blank expressions. The air buzzes with moaning. The metallic reek of blood invades her nostrils.

She walks among the sheet-covered mounds but cannot bring herself to look under any of them. Tom talks with a railway worker who is helping to carry bodies to a wagon. Usually, this man sells the train tickets. He and Tom nod and wave. Lottie's innards flutter. Tom strides towards her. His smile beaming through the grimy tear tracks makes him look more grisly than when he is dismayed.

'Good news, Mrs Turner,' Tom says. 'Your husband took the tickets back this morning for a refund. He wasn't on the train.'

Lottie's legs turn to rubber. She slumps to the grass in a phoof of billowing skirts and apron fabric. Tom kneels beside her, the picture of concern. Lottie tries to shake off her dread. She's received the news that so many around her would give anything to receive right now.

George is alive.

Where is George?

Lottie knows where he is, where he took the cash. She knows that by the end of the day there will be not one penny left.

Lottie presses her thumb into her bruised rib, buries her face in her apron and lets the weeping wash over her.

The Armagh rail disaster happened on 12 June 1889. Eighty people were killed and 260 injured, about a third of them children. It was the worst rail disaster in the UK in the nineteenth century, and remains Ireland's worst railway disaster ever.

Byddi Lee writes novels, flash fiction, and short stories. She co-founded Flash Fiction Armagh, and co-edits *The Bramley – An Anthology of Flash Fiction Armagh.* Along with two other members of the Armagh Theatre Group, Byddi wrote *IMPACT – Armagh's Train Disaster* which was staged in June 2019 in the Abbey Lane Theatre in Armagh.

Portadown Pixies and Paint Pots
Lorna Flanagan

Mischief took it into her head to paint the town red.

With a twinkle in his eye, *Sexy Rexy* said, 'Why just the town? Why not the countryside? C'mon, we'll paint it red too while we're at it.'

Then *Oranges and Lemons* chimed in. 'Why only red? Give it some zest. Splash a bit of orange and lemon about as well.'

The Pixies of Portadown were a busy wee bunch. Normally, behind the scenes, they acted as cheerleaders to the linen weavers, the curers of ham and bacon, the packers of eggs, butter, poultry, and apples. They revived the spirits of the people who worked in the flourmills and the iron and brass foundries. And they did the same for those who looked after the steam locomotives, carriages, and wagons in the Great Northern Railway marshalling yards at the junction station.

No one knew the Pixies were there, but their mischievous sense of fun kept morale high during the long factory hours. And when, one day, *Mischief* came across a few tins of red paint, she thought of a different way to brighten things up. But it had to be done when no one was looking.

That evening, when the humans had gone home, *Mischief*, *Sexy Rexy*, and *Oranges and Lemons* trooped out to the edge of the town, together with *Singin' in the Rain*, *Portadown Fragrance*,

Ice White, *Silent Night*, and lots of their friends, all carrying pots of paint and brushes.

When darkness fell, *Ice White* and *Silent Night* went ahead of the others and scattered stardust so the rest could see as they painted. *Mischief* painted a thick flame-red line along the edge of the first field from one corner to the other. *Sexy Rexy* followed with a long wide stripe of dark red, next to *Mischief*'s line. *Oranges and Lemons* added thick streaks of lemon and orange. One by one the other Pixies carried on with deep salmon pink, apricot, cream, white, yellow, copper, and delicate pastels until the whole field was covered. Then they did the same with the next field, and the next, and the one after that, until dawn was approaching.

Just before sunrise, *Ice White* and *Silent Night* packed away what was left of the stardust. *Singin' in the Rain* and *Portadown Fragrance* hid in the hedgerows because they had extra plans. The others gathered up the brushes and empty tins and took them back into town.

A sudden thought struck *Mischief*. 'Argh,' she said, 'We've had so much fun we forgot to do the town. Oh well, too late now.'

They all sneaked into an old store in the foundry, huddled together, and waited. From their hiding place, they heard some folk trudging in for the early morning shift.

One of the humans who lived on the outskirts shouted, 'The fields are on fire! The countryside's ablaze!'

But nobody believed him. No smoke? No fire. Back to work.

The sun rose higher in the sky, and spread summer heat everywhere. *Singin' in the Rain* emerged from his hiding place in the hedge and flew around the fields, scattering raindrops over the warm ground. *Portadown Fragrance* fluttered after him and sprayed a selection of her perfumes in all directions.

With the potent blend of sunshine, warm fertile soil, rain, and scent, the painted stripes came alive. A magic spark ran through the vibrant streaks that swept across the undulating landscape. The multi-coloured fields pulsated with life and began to produce flowers — but not just any kind of flower. They were roses, the Queen of Flowers.

The people of the town were amazed. There were gasps of wonder and admiration.

'Would you just take a look at that!'

'The whole countryside's a blaze of colour!'

'Fire with no smoke! Now we know what you mean!'

Even the Pixies themselves couldn't have imagined anything like this, when they set out to brighten things up. But at that time they hadn't yet heard of Sam McGredy's roses. And what would they have thought of his hand painted ones, like *Old Master*, the rose with a white centre splashed on its crimson petals?

As *Mischief* says, 'You never know what'll happen when you take a notion to paint the town red.'

Lorna Flanagan was born in Portadown. Moved away. Now back again and re-inspired by the energy and creativity of many local family enterprises like Portadown's internationally renowned rose breeders, and in particular by Sam McGredy's playful names for some of his award-winning roses. He died in 2019 and this is a tribute.

Glorious and Grand
Adeline Henry

'Place' is a dangerous word. In this part of the world, it can smack of all the tweeness of 'The Wee Six' and 'our wee province', the folksy terms that Northern Irish natives – some of them – assign to it.

I grew up in rural County Armagh, towards the south of the county, but I wouldn't have called it South Armagh. This term was used in the media but not by people in the Protestant community that I knew.

As a child, I played games with my sisters and cousins, games of secret clubs, with passwords and membership badges. I was the wonderful, and entirely imaginary, *Carlotta Rivers*. For my membership badge, I cut out a picture of a woman from a magazine. She was tall, elegant and smart, and worked as a detective.

Our club had a song. It might have been the only song I knew that wasn't a hymn: *The Boys from the County Armagh*. Members of our club had to learn it off by heart. I can still remember all the words. It comes to mind at strange times, and I've found myself singing it at the top of my voice in the car, a strange panacea to the anxiety of having an elderly parent in hospital.

'There's one fair county in Ireland,' it goes. Around here,

counties are important. Depending on who you're talking to, sometimes there are six of them and sometimes there are 32; numbers matter. Back then, we all knew that County Armagh was the best, certainly never County Down. That place was a strange land, found on the other side of the Newry to Banbridge Road, and full of hardy farming people who knew how to whitewash and keep things tidy. They were the kind that ended up in places like Carolina or Tennessee, ancestors of US presidents, the sort of people you wouldn't want to cross.

County Armagh has a soft edge to it, a homely quality, summed up in soft, green, rounded hills contoured with hedges and dotted with scraps of woolly white. It is at its best in Spring, when the whin is most yellow and fragrant, and the hawthorn is delicate and white, like a bridal veil. Then, the sun shines warmly from blue skies, the daffodils and crocuses bring colour back to the borders of our lane, and it feels like hope.

I come from Crieve, a tiny townland with only three houses, which seemed to my child's mind to be the epicentre of County Armagh's abundance. Our storey-and-a-half stone farmhouse had been built by my grandfather and his brothers. It was the original homeplace, although the family moved to another farm nearby. My Dad, the second son, inherited the farm and moved in after he got married. The house nestled under our hill – the highest part of the farm – and we prided ourselves on having a vantage point over south Armagh, right out to Black Bank, Dead Man's Hill, and Newtownhamilton.

Our land edged Lough Gilly, at its foot. It was too boggy to venture near the lough. Cattle sometimes got stuck in the soft ground at the edge of drains down there. Some years ago, Dad struck up conversation with a group of archaeologists who were excavating the site of a bomb in Armagh, and brought them home. They told him there was a prehistoric crannog – a man-made island – in the lough, now no longer separate from the shore. He dreamed of a tourist trail, maybe by donkey and cart, from the ancient burial site – a barrow, they told him – at the farm's highest point, to the lough at its lowest. That was before farm diversification, when farmers were encouraged to find means of income from their land, other than from farming activity.

There's an idyllic pastoral tint to my memories here that belies other recollections: the sight of a soldier, lying on his belly under a hedge, looking through the sights of his rifle, or reports of a man's body, lying in a ditch, or the terror of visiting family in Bandit Country, and wondering if we'd be safe on the road home.

Sometimes, in the summers of the 70's and 80's, the English aunts came 'home'. Embarrassingly, they would insist on kissing us children on the cheek. There were parties, old-style, with men in one room and women in another. Whiskey and sherry were served, and a full-scale supper was presented at half past ten at night, with sandwiches, cakes, buns and tarts.

After supper, the socialising would be mixed; there'd be a blurry quality to proceedings, and that's when one aunt would usually suggest a song. *Danny Boy* was a favourite, but it went too high. War time songs like *It's a Long Way to Tipperary* would rouse the sleepy. Of course, the one that always got the loudest rendition was *The Boys from the County Armagh*. When it came to the second verse, we got ready for 'round by the gap of Mountnorris', at which point we all whooped and cheered for our local village.

At home time, hours past my normal bedtime, the women would drive, and the men would slump askew in the passenger seat.

We'd drive home under the moonlight. I'd look out the window of the car, feeling safe, seeing but not being seen by the world, and feeling tired and full from the bond of belonging.

Adeline Henry is from Co Armagh. She has worked as a translator, and as a teacher of languages and yoga. Following completion of the MA in Creative Writing at Queens University Belfast, in 2019 she was awarded a Creative Writing PhD scholarship at Ulster University to write her first novel.

City of Belfast

Belfast is replete with literary talent, showcased by a group of ten Women Aloud NI writers - wordsmiths of prose and poetry. The city's section kicks off with a colourful 'lullaby' to Belfast by acclaimed crime author, **Sharon Dempsey**, *who brings a difficult period in Northern Ireland's history to life within the context of ordinary lives, and a filial love that carried on regardless.*

Aislin O'Neill *continues the theme, in a tale which examines mother/daughter strife and has a bloody denouement.*

Clare McWilliams *has written one of her powerful poems, Take Me Home a Thousand Times, and she is followed by another poet,* **Anita Gracey**, *who takes over, in a poetic pause, with her Virginia Woolf-inspired piece.*

Wilma Kenny's *first poem, Leaving home, leads us towards* **Linda Hutchinson**, *with her story steeped in nostalgia. A second poem by* **Wilma Kenny** *is followed by* **Ellie Rose McKee's** *humorous slice of Belfast life, overflowing with the trademark Belfast wit and vernacular.*

Gaynor Kane *takes us back in time to the building of the Titanic, while* **Rosie Burrows** *gives us a soulful epistolary to her baby grandson. Finally,* **Alison Black** *brings the city's chapter to a close with a poem entitled A Victim No More.*

A Belfast Lullaby
Sharon Dempsey

'For fuck's sake are we to listen to that carry on tonight again?'

Da's not impressed. The rabid republicans, as he calls them, are out in force. One of the hunger strikers must have died, for there's a rattle of bin lids echoing up the entries. A war cry of metal on concrete, bouncing off brick walls and cascading its way into his bones.

'Them wee fuckers are doing my head in. I can't get peace in my own house.'

Our Jonny sits watching the television, rocking back and forth. He does that when he's happy. He does it when he's sad too, but at the minute I think he's happy.

'Jesus wept for your troubles. Would you not give a moment's thought to the poor craiter who's just died?' Ma offers, with a cigarette half-hanging out of her mouth. She's sewing our Jonny's trousers – they're too long and his legs are too short.

'Poor craiter my arse. Choosing to die for the cause doesn't mean he's a martyr, just a fucking fool. Dirty campaign, my arse. Fucking ridiculous. Maggie Thatcher's laughing at the lot of them.'

I snigger. Da's hilarious when he goes off on one.

The miners' strike, EEC butter mountains, the price of petrol, the state of the nation stuff. He revels in it. Once he nearly had a stroke going on about privatisation. He had himself so worked up that he burst a blood vessel in his eyeball. Dr Hunt had a look at it and told him that his blood pressure was too high. Ma said if he didn't wise up, he'd be dead before the next election. We didn't have the news on for two days after that.

'Give over, and higher up the TV,' Ma says, the ash on the end of her cigarette reaching that droop stage, when you know it's going to fall. She ignores it and keeps on sewing while watching the television, her eyes squinting against the smoke. Jonny hates the smell of it so he's staying at his end of the room. They have an arrangement. She never blows the smoke in his direction.

We sit in expectation waiting to hear what the newsreader will say, even though the jungle drums of the entries have already told us. Another one of the hunger strikers has died. The city is alight with riots. There's probably one kicking off at the top of the road. Milk bottles, full of amber petrol will be raining down on the Brits. If we're quiet, we can probably hear them. The roar and the clatter. The sirens and the crack of a plastic bullet going off. The cheer of the crowd.

I look across at Jonny. His big wonky face is doughy and childlike. If you pinch his cheeks, he laughs like it's the funniest thing ever. He's picking his nose. Mining for gold, as Ma would say. In a world of his own. The bin lids and petrol bombs mean nothing to him. His world begins and stops here, in this house. Sometimes I wonder what will happen to him. After, I mean. After Ma and Da are dead, buried in Milltown with the rabid republicans for neighbours.

'What's it? Jonny asks.

He's caught me looking and I smile at him. That's all he

58

needs. If I smile, it makes him happy. Maybe I'll take him with me when I go. I know I won't, but it's nice to pretend. To imagine that he can tag along with me to Manchester or Liverpool or wherever it is I end up. He could keep house. Have the dinner waiting on me coming in. He can heat up beans in a pan and make a bit of toast. They taught him that at his special school. He got a certificate and kept the apron, even though he wasn't supposed to.

One time I asked granny why Jonny was so much older than me. Everyone else has brothers and sisters close in age. Granny said it was because Ma and Da had to be sure they'd get the next one right.

'You know not every brother would be as good to him as you are. God sent you to look out for him. He's a harmless gobshite with no sense in his head, but he's our gobshite, so we have to take care of him.'

I love him, but that day I realised I was meant to be the one to look after him when the rest of them are gone. Maybe I wouldn't have been born if they didn't need me to mind Jonny. When Eamonn McClure from around the corner called Jonny a spastic, I busted his lip. Da told me I shouldn't have reacted. Should have kept my cool and walked away, but when Ma got me in the kitchen, she said I did the right thing, sticking up for Jonny. She slipped me a couple of quid, the green notes tucked into my hand, and said, 'Here, get yourself a wee treat from the shop.'

When Jonny turned eighteen, we had a party in the house. All the aunts and uncles came and the wee cousins too even though Jonny doesn't like them. When it was time to bring out the cake granny had baked, I went into the kitchen and found Ma crying. 'What's the matter?' I said, even though I didn't really want to know. Mas shouldn't be crying, especially not over birthday cakes. 'Awk it's just that eighteen's a big age. He should be a man but he's still my baby.'

I didn't want to point out that I was technically the baby of the family.

The news is over and we're getting ready for bed. The back door is locked, and the television is turned off at the plug.

'Right, night then,' says Da. We pretend we're the Waltons and everyone says night, night, before heading up the stairs.

Ma makes sure Jonny brushes his teeth and then tells him to put on his pyjamas. He doesn't like getting changed. Doesn't see why we put something different on, just to go to bed. I can see his point. Me and Jonny still share a room. He doesn't like the dark and he doesn't like sleeping on his own. I don't mind. I've the top bunk.

When he's in his flannel, brown and orange check pyjamas, he kneels down and says his prayers. He asks Jesus to bless us all and keep us safe from the dark, then lumbers into his bottom bunk. Sometimes he lifts his big, thick legs and kicks my mattress, lifting me clean up, close enough to touch the ceiling but tonight he's too tired for that carry on.

The house settles into itself for the night. Jonny's asleep as soon as his head hits the pillow. He snores and talks in his sleep. I'm used to it. When I move away, I'll probably miss the sound of him in the bunk below me.

The bin lid racket has died down and all I can hear is distant traffic and the whirr of an overhead helicopter. I don't mind it. Da says it's a Belfast lullaby. I wonder what sounds I'll hear at night when I'm across the water and if Jonny will learn to sleep on his own.

Sharon Dempsey's crime debut, *Little Bird*, was published to critical acclaim in 2017. She has also published two women's fiction novels and is working on a new crime series, along with a modern day Gothic standalone thriller. She writes plays and short stories and is a creative writing tutor at Queen's. She is represented by the Kate Nash Literary Agency.

Confirmation
Aislin O'Neill

'I can't wait 'til tomorrow.' Annie was making the most of break-time, sharing a bag of rainbow drops with her best friend, Kathleen, and discussing the plans for her big day out. They took it in turns to slowly suck the chemically-charged fluorescent colour off each individual rice puff before showing their tongues to each other.

Annie's mind had been oblivious to anything else ever since her mum had promised a shopping trip into town to buy a brand-new confirmation dress. New clothes were a rare experience for Annie. As the youngest of eight, she'd been condemned to a wardrobe of items her sister had grown out of. However, Bridie – although only two years older than Annie – was big for her age. The prospect of a Saturday shopping trip into Belfast, just for her, had filled her every thought since her mum had told her the weekend before. It would be a chance to choose something other than Bridie's old Sunday frock, which had very obviously been made for a sturdier and taller girl.

Spring term had put all the P6 class at St Michael's Primary school in a state of high excitement. Aged nine, going on ten, they were grown-up enough to recommit their faith in God and the Church. Most of the term had been given over to preparation for the sacrament of Confirmation, including twice weekly visits from the principal, filling their heads with stories of hell and damnation.

Break-time discussions, though, had become all about what they were going to wear for the big day. For weeks, Annie had sat silently on the edge of the chatter, until her mother's unexpected promise had made the gossip wonderfully relevant to her too.

'So, do you think you'll get your Ma to buy you that cream dress with the orange, flowery sleeves?' Kathleen's eye for fashion always made Annie jealous. Other than sneaked peeks at Bridie's weekly *Jackie magazine*, Annie really didn't have a clue, and relied on her best friend to keep her straight.

'I'm going to try.' Annie looked again at a picture of a dress that Kathleen had cut out for her from the Belfast Telegraph. The image, now crisscrossed with faded fold marks, was hard to make out, but Annie stared at it dreamily. The dress was from British Home Stores; she really hoped she could steer her Ma in that direction.

They'd been late setting off. Annie's brother had decided to be sick after breakfast – she suspected he'd done it to spite her, because of the beating he'd gotten after Annie told on him for eating the last Garibaldi biscuit. Any guilt she'd felt for touting on him disappeared when she realised they would miss the twelve-thirty bus, jeopardising the pre-shopping lunch out Annie had been hoping for.

'Hurry up. We haven't got all day. Pick up your feet, girl.'

This wasn't how it was supposed to be; running late, her Ma in a mood. It was meant to be special. Annie wanted to be special. This was meant to be her day.

'We'll still be able to go for lunch, Ma, won't we?'

She willed her mum to smile at her, to say everything would go as planned, to make things okay. But she didn't.

'Ma, we can, can't we?'

The unease grew bigger in Annie's belly, that sick feeling, never far from the surface when dealing with her Ma. The not knowing which Ma she was dealing with.

Ma said nothing.

The one o'clock bus was packed. Glancing sideways, Annie tried to measure her mother's mood. A thunder of possible conversations exploded in her head. She stayed quiet. Better no word than the wrong word.

A girl got on at the next stop, wearing a skirt short enough to draw a disgusted tut from Annie's Ma. The girl turned at the sound, lips painted bright red, with a gaze that settled briefly on Ma before moving on.

"Wee hussy! Can't be more than fourteen," Ma hissed.

Annie envied the girl her freedom. She wished - not for the first time - that *she* was fourteen, and could escape. Fourteen held possibilities that nine could only yearn for.

'Ma, we're here.' Annie searched her mum's face for clues as to who she might be dealing with.

'Looks like it's a busy one. Here, Annie. You hold my basket.'

Annie sighed inwardly, giddy with relief. This felt normal.

'Right, we'll head to Woolworths, first; see what they have in the sale. I haven't got money to burn.'

Annie suppressed a reflex niggle of disappointment, determined to keep everything on an even keel. She was used to navigating this ship.

'Okay, Ma. That sounds good,' she lied with well-practiced conviction. The shame she would feel if her classmates found out her dress had come from Woolworths didn't bear thinking about. The trick was going to be getting her mother to British Home Stores, while making her think it was her idea.

'Are we going to have lunch first, Ma?' Annie tentatively broached her other ambition for the day. Having left the house later than planned, but too early for lunch, her stomach was already conducting a symphony of hunger.

'No. We're too late for lunch. If you'd walked a bit quicker, we might have had time.'

Annie stayed quiet, allowing the mis-apportioned blame to settle comfortably on her narrow shoulders.

Woolworths proved fruitless. Then, trawling around Little-woods, her Ma had forced Annie to try on two monstrosities: a sea of net and frill more suited to a five-year old than a grown-up girl of nine had reinforced Annie's determination. Her efforts to resist the urge to whinge or sound ungrateful at each unsuitable garment finally reaped their due reward with a visit to BHS.

Dress bag clutched in her hand and glowing with success, Annie finally let a hint of a whine slip into her voice.

'Ma, I'm really starving. Can we *please* get something to eat? You did say we would, just the two of us.' She figured it was worth the risk of pushing for the icing on the cake.

'We've food in the house. We got what we came for; now we're going for the bus. Hurry up, for God's sake.'

'But, Ma, you said we could go to a restaurant. You promised. We missed lunch. Can we not go for our tea? Please Ma, please!' Desperation heightened the hunger pangs Annie had ignored in her crusade for the perfect dress.

Hurrying through Corn Market, struggling to keep up, Annie saw the sign. Kathleen had told her that the Abercorn was the place to go.

'Look, Ma. We could go in there.'

Kathleen's older sister, Maeve, was fifteen, and she'd gone to the upstairs bar with her boyfriend, Sean. Kathleen had been to the downstairs restaurant four times with her mum.

'Ma, please. Let's go here. You could have a cup of tea; I'll just have a milk. We don't even have to eat. Ma, please?' The need for an experience to impress her friend outweighed Annie's fear of her Ma's response. 'Please Ma, please.'

'Stop your whining, Annie, or I'll give you something to whine about,' her Ma spat out, but she did stop to examine the menu in the window of the restaurant.

Annie held her breath.

'Okay, we can go in. Don't think it's because I've given in to you, Miss Annie. It's because I need the toilet.'

Annie said nothing, but, as her mum turned away, she couldn't stop her lips widening in a grin of triumph.

Chicken and chips in a basket – that's what Kathleen had told her about in their break-time chats. That was what you had to get.

'Okay let's find a seat then, missy. I'm not giving in, mind. I feel a bit peckish myself, so don't you go thinking you can get your way if you whinge enough. That won't work with me, you hear me, Annie?'

'Yes, Ma.' Annie kept her expression dutifully grateful as they threaded their way through the crowded restaurant to a table by the window. She placed the bag with her new dress inside carefully beside her on the seat, where she could see it and be sure of not forgetting it.

Half an hour later, Annie was licking her fingers and savouring the last traces of greasy saltiness from her chicken and chips, while she watched two teenagers sitting a few tables away. She'd been absent-mindedly studying them while her mother chatted throughout the meal. Both girls had kept their coats on, as if they weren't stopping long. She liked the look of one girl's expensive-looking red leather handbag.

'Hurry up and finish, Annie. We haven't got all day.'

Ma broke in on Annie's day-dream of owning a bag like that when she was older, and free.

'Can we get some ice cream, Ma?' She knew she was really pushing her luck, now, but Kathleen had said the Abercorn's knickerbocker glories were to die for, and Annie wanted one. She crossed her fingers under the table, held her breath and smiled her best smile at her Ma.

The giant ice cream arrived. She glanced over at the girls, but they had gone, and the waitress was leading a different pair of young women to the empty table. The two friends laughed as they shoved their shopping under the table and eagerly picked up the menu. Annie glimpsed a flash of red leather amongst the shopping bags. Had the previous girl left her handbag behind?

Annie coughed on dust – thick dust coating the air. Her tongue stuck to the roof of her mouth. She tried to swallow the dribble of spit she had left, to clear her throat. Her eyes stung.

Her gaze fell on the long-handled spoon in her hand. There had been a knickerbocker glory, hadn't there? She'd had just one spoonful of the ice-cream. Where was the rest of it? Where was her dress? She looked around searching for the BHS bag she'd put on the seat beside her. But she wasn't on the seat anymore – she was on the floor. She couldn't see her bag. She had to find her dress. She'd be in so much trouble if it was ruined. Ma would kill her if she'd lost it.

Why was she on the floor?

'Ma, where are you?' The dust clogging her throat made the words little more than a rasp. She tried again. 'Ma! Ma, where are you?'

Strange groaning and muffled crying – not unlike the sound her dog, Molly, had made when she'd whelped her seven pups in the garden shed – grew in intensity, cutting through the ringing in her ears.

'Annie?' Her Ma's voice came small and fragile, not like Ma at all.

Annie stretched her hands out searching through the grey fog. 'Ma? Where are you, Ma? I can't see you.' She felt her way towards the voice, through the dust cloud, across a floor covered in unseen fragments, bits of wood, glass that scrunched under foot, and sometimes something softer, wetter.

Panic rose in her throat, but she held it in. She was a big girl, too old to cry, especially in public. The dusty shroud slowly dissipated, and the broken scene it revealed drove all thoughts of the dress from Annie's mind. She just wanted to find her Ma.

'Annie! I'm here.' Annie grabbed at the hand sticking out from beneath a broken, upturned table.

'Ma!'

'It's okay, Annie. I'm okay.' The harsh certainty to her mother's voice had gone. Instead her words quivered with emotion and something Annie hadn't heard before.

Ma was crying.

'It's okay, Ma. I'm here. Don't worry.' The hand tightened its grip and Annie let her own tears fall.

The Abercorn Restaurant was bombed on 4 March 1972. The bomb explosion claimed the lives of two young women and injured over 130 people. Many of the injuries were severe. No one was ever charged in connection with the bombing.

A ten-week writing course inspired **Aislin O'Neill** to pursue an MA in Creative Writing at Queen's University Belfast, from which she graduated with Distinction in 2019. Her writing focus is on noir and auto-fiction, with mother-daughter relationships being a particular interest. She is working on her first novel – *'Unknown Pleasures.'*

Take Me Home A Thousand Times
Clare McWilliams

The door hisses and I taste the breath of you hungrily.
The umami of damp oil and needless pessimism
pervades my tongue
as I step back into you.

The belief that nothing happens here that's good
Sweats the air, with years of conditioning
Entrenchment and staleness.
Keep the shirt your father wore,
Shhhhhh.
Just wear it underneath yourself.
The need to:
Get out,
Get drunk,
Wise up.
Get skilled,
Get lucky,
Get away,
Far away.
Is Gone Now.
Flipped to a
Here is me,

Here is wee,
Here C'mere,
I am Home.
All that I love is here.
Green and Basalt bodies with linen tops
Soothe my misty eyes.
The loamy scent of you defines my marshy past.
The pain of you strengthens me, lengthens me,
Stands me up tall in the ancient reins of you.

I scuttle back to the city in a, too big for some bridges,
Bus.
I click clack carefully across the cobbles
of the Cathedral Quarter,
Catching faces that mirror their mother's
endless windchange warnings
Long ago,
When the blood of you was young
and fresh full of rage.
I look away to the walls, tagged
With transient new normals,
Stretching up to an
Ever-decreasing
Triangle of
Grey.
I bop into The Sunflower for a drink.
It's quiet in the garden today and I get a good bit of my
cryptic done.
Just the one, eh?
Two would be folly with a suitcase in tow.
There's no craic to argue with me.
I nip into the toilets and wish,

Again,
That I could write my poetry all over them.
Get over yourself, you sing in my ear.
My Pride My Joy My Fear My Shame
All come from you.
My Helter-Skelter life mimics yours,
A state still forming.
Up Royal Avenue I strut; and duck in quick to grab a bite.
Scoot straight to City Hall.
Where segregated subcultures sit,
plotted on the lawn like stone daisies.
Silent, unscripted, reality shows
With greedy gulls guzzling scraps.
Suddenly,
High above your domes and spires, craning to be felt,
Soothing hunched shoulders like fiery balm,
lashing smiles on bakes,
All on the lawn unite
and lift their chins
To the Glory Ana* in Our Sky.

*Ana- Celtic Deity- The primordial goddess of Nature
Divine mother of the supernatural tribe of all the Celtic Gods and Goddesses

Clare McWilliams is a poet, spoken word artist, playwright and a poetry facilitator. Originally from Bangor, and shaped by the sea, she now resides in Belfast. She is currently devising and rehearsing a new show, with thanks to funding by the Arts Council of NI and the National Lottery.

Avant-Garden
Anita Gracey

"A woman must have money and a room
of her own if she is to write fiction."
A Room of One's Own, 1929, extended essay by Virginia Woolf

As the weightiest sun pours
it leads me to a deck chair

cloud curl locks my hair
distant traffic stays distant

breeze whispers my skin
goosebumps pout lips

Cryptic Wood White's dance
sweet pea exudes a trance

hornets retire to hollows
chaffinch cradles a lullaby

young grass loses their vigour
wet-the-bed parachute down

carefree lopper yawn
hosepipe drip countdown

my eyelids heavy, heavier, heaviest
Virginia Woolf tumbles from grasp

one's own liberty
my garden reverie.

Anita Gracey has been published in Poetry Ireland Review amongst others. Anita was featured in *The Poetry Jukebox* and shortlisted *Chultúrlann 2020*. Anita is supported by an iDA award, managed by the University of Atypical on behalf of the Arts Council of Northern Ireland.

Leaving Home
Wilma Kenny

Not looking back, I left the place where sheep
are hefted to the mountain. My friend, her dad
the last working shepherd, came with me.

I ran carefree to the popping corn of gunfire;
here boys patrolled Belfast streets,
with rifles as big as themselves.

Wilma Kenny's poems and short stories have been published in a
number of anthologies and journals, recently, in *Open Ear* and *Answer
the Call (Whiskey and Words)*. She was the winner of the Waterford Writ-
ers Poetry Competition in 2018 and the 2019 winner of the Dalkey
Creates poetry competition.

The Davy Crockett Gang
Linda Hutchinson

Ronnie liked Fridays because it was pocket money day; he'd no homework and Crackerjack was on TV. But there was no doubt that Saturday was the best day of the week. Ronnie wolfed down his Weetabix and grabbed his cowboy hat and cap gun on his way out to play in the street. The gang met at the corner lamppost and the first there could swing on the rope the big lads had put up.

Ronnie swung and savoured the day ahead. He never missed a week at the Roy Rogers Club at the Mercury Cinema. He thought about the Club Rules: be clean and tidy, courteous and polite, obey your parents, protect the weak and most importantly, be brave and never take chances.

'Bout ye, oul son.' Derek strolled up. He liked to be called Deke, that was his cowboy name. Big Jimbo was right behind him. 'We'd better call for Hank or we'll be late.'

They rapped the knocker of number six.

'Hello, Mrs Watson. Is Hank coming out?'

She looked at them as if she had a bad smell under her nose.

'Henry will be out shortly.' She closed the door.

The three lads looked at each other and giggled.

When Hank appeared, they stopped sniggering. He was wearing none other than a Davy Crockett hat.

'Where'd you get that?' said Deke, open-mouthed.

'Dad got me it, just in time for the film on Thursday.'

'It's wheeker.' The boys were suitably impressed.

'Now, we are officially the Davy Crockett Gang and I'm the leader.'

'How come you're the leader?'

'Cos I have the hat.'

Ronnie was quiet. He was getting a racoon hat for his birthday but that was two months away. Lots of the kids would have one for Thursday night, but in his family they only got presents for Christmas and birthdays. He hoped Davy Crockett was still popular by the time he got his hat.

The gang made their way to join the unruly crowd of children congregating outside the Mercury. As ten-year-olds, they were head and shoulders above most of the others and easily jostled their way to the top of the queue, only to be stopped in their tracks by Frankie, the commissionaire, their old adversary.

'Oi. Back of the line you boys. I seen you bumping the queue.'

'No, sir,' said Hank in his best innocent little boy voice. 'That's my sister, sir, she was keeping my place, sir.'

'I know you, Henry Watson. You'd better behave yourself this week or you're barred.'

'Yes, sir. No problem sir.'

Frankie wore a military style jacket and hat, dusty maroon with gold braid. From under his hat, a wig of dark curls peeped out. He strode along the crowd of kids, trying to coax them into an orderly queue.

'Oi Frankie, who knit your wig?' came a cry from the crowd, causing a burst of laughter.

Frankie swung round, 'I'm watching you, Watson.'

Just then the doors opened and there was a mad scramble as everyone tried to squeeze in together, regardless of their place in the line. Ten minutes of chaos followed, when tickets, sweeties and sticky lollies were bought.

In the front stalls, the children cheered and shouted as they found seats and settled down for their Saturday entertainment. On to the screen came Roy Rogers himself, mounted on his golden palomino, Trigger, the white fringes on his shirt swaying as he rode. The children cheered at the sight of their hero, but silence reigned when he started to speak. He greeted the audience, dismounted and invited them to bow their heads for the Cowboy's prayer. Every head in the Mercury was bowed as Roy asked the Lord to help them all to follow the rules and be good.

Then the show began. There was a Bugs Bunny cartoon, an episode of the cowboy serial, Texas Gunslingers, an Abbott and Costello comedy and some trailers for upcoming features at the cinema. The boys were interested in one for Tarzan's Hidden Jungle, then everybody booed at the trailer for Oklahoma.

My Mum would love that, thought Ronnie, with all that singing and dancing.

Then what they had all been hoping for – the trailer for the new Disney movie, Davy Crockett and the River Pirates. Cheers, whistles, clapping and stamping greeted the sight of Davy on screen, so much so that they couldn't hear the words.

Never mind, thought Ronnie, we'll be here on opening night to see it in glorious technicolour.

Trailers over, there was a rush and a crush for the doors again, despite the best efforts of Frankie and usherette Janis to hold them back.

Outside, there was the usual burst of gunfire as cap guns

went off with whoops and cheers, until Frankie chased the kids away with a growl. The boys usually made their way to the park, but today Hank gathered them together in a huddle and whispered, 'Wait 'til you see what else I've got. C'mon down the entry.'

Intrigued, the gang followed their leader down the alley at the side of the picture house, where, to their surprise, Hank pulled four Park Drive and some matches out of his pocket. They were stunned.

'Where'd you get them?' said Deke in a hushed tone.

'From my ma's handbag. She'll never miss them,' boasted Hank. 'Here, one each.' He handed round the fags and the others stared at the small white objects in their hands.

'I'm not sure about this,' said Ronnie. 'What would Roy say?'

'He's not here, is he? But if you're too scaredy to have a go, you can give it back.'

Ronnie handed the cigarette back and was turning to leave when he saw Frankie spying on them. He must have followed them.

Frankie barged into the middle of the group just in time to see Hank drop the cigarettes and run off.

'It was him, mister. We never done nothing.' Deke seemed to have forgotten about loyalty to the gang.

'I knew he was up to something. He's for it this time.'

The boys hurried home, glad to be off the hook.

Thursday came round at last and excitement was mounting. Ronnie could hardly swallow his tea, but shovelled in the last bits so Mum would let him leave the table. Dad was taking him to the film that night. He loved going to the pictures with Dad. They had gone to see The Dambusters and Ronnie played at shooting down planes for weeks after. Dad always got them Kia-Ora at the interval.

'Just before we go, I have a surprise for you, son. You've been a good lad and you deserve it. Call it an early birthday present.'

Mum handed him a Davy Crockett hat. His eyes widened.

'Oh boy,' he shouted. 'King of the Wild Frontier.'

'Come on, Davy,' said Dad. 'We have some river pirates to deal with.'

The queue at the Mercury was long but much more well-behaved than on Saturday mornings. Kids stood quietly with their parents. Ronnie spotted Jimbo with his family and waved to him.

'Beezer hat,' Jimbo yelled.

Up ahead at the ticket office, there seemed to be something going on. Ronnie craned his neck to see and realised it was Frankie talking to Hank's Mum and Dad and waggling his finger at a very sorry-looking Hank.

'Right,' said Mr Watson, pulling Hank out of the line by the ear and grabbing the racoon hat from his head. 'No tickets for us, thanks. We're going home.'

Ronnie watched as Hank slunk away with his parents, then turned to his own Dad.

'Okay son, let's get two for the back stalls and a couple of choc ices. We're gonna have a great night.'

Linda Hutchinson is proud to call herself a member of Women Aloud NI. She owes much to fellow members, who have encouraged and supported her as a writer. She is currently working on her second historical novel for children. She also loves to write short stories, particularly those that celebrate her Belfast childhood.

8, Arlington Road
Wilma Kenny

We try to be respectable,
run a tidy, clean house
for tidy, clean people,
cook a standard, no choice,
take it or leave it breakfast.

Then I get a visit from the council.
The git comes in and says:
"We've had a complaint."
A woman who came from Newry
to visit her wee lad in hospital.
Right enough, I remember the night.
She was in the room next to the
big tart from Fermanagh
who brings back the fellas
she picks up outside the Europa.
I'm all red in the face as I tell him,
"We try to keep a respectable house."

Stress Response
Ellie Rose McKee

"…it was just a bog-standard GP appointment. I thought I'd be in and out, handed some pills or a sticking plaster and bing, bang, bosh, Bob's yer uncle.

But no, apparently not.

I'd been having these headaches, see? Real blinding, like. My guts had been kicking up a fuss for at least a week, and I was covered — absolutely bleeding blighted — with sores. The doc said they were cold sores, but they didn't feel all that chilly to me so I'm not so sure on that count. The big thing, though, that was the kicker.

Stress, she said. The whole lot of it, down to stress. Can you believe it? I said she was having a laugh. I don't believe in this 'stress' nonsense.

But the headaches? I said.

She said stress.

Fine, I said, willing to let that one go. But the dicky tummy?

Stress, she said again.

It was real clear to me then that she was a header. I shoulda known when I first walked in and seen one of them-there dream catchers hangin' on the windee – blowin' in the wind like a fart in a trance, it was – but there was abso-tootly no doubting now. She was cuckoo.

Stress must be one of those-there biz words that's all the rage, just like cancer was before, y'know? They used to say everything was cancer, or that ACDC bollocks.

Anyway. So, these 'cold sores,' says I, what's with them?

And then I stopped her as soon as I asked, 'cause she got that look in her eye and I knew right there and then that she was gonna say stress again. I shook my head and said to myself, I'll go and see a real doctor next time.

A bloke's not gonna fob me off, I think to myself. I'll grin and bear it, find out what she suggests for 'stress,' go on me merry way an' re-book fer the next week.

Now, this is where she near knocked me down. What was the prescription? Flippin' *meditation*. Some other hippy-dippy shite.

I guess she could tell I wasn't buyin' it, because she tried again t' get me on side. The real solution, says she, is to find the *source* of the stress and deal with it. Well, that just buttered my crumpet, I can tell ye. I walked out, thinking she was a right wingnut. But d'ya know what? I couldn't get this here stress idea outta my head.

I was thinking on it, see. And I wasn't ready to try that mediation nonsense or whatall, but I had one of those wee — what're they called — thunderstorms, but in yer head, like? Can't remember the name, but no matter – one of those.

What have I got to be stressed about? says me to myself. And I thought, this upcoming holiday seems a bit of a to-do. So, I cancelled it, got right back to work, and I've been right as rain since.

These doctors, I tell ya. Not worth the time. Sure, I was better just sorting myself.

Anyway. Thanks, pal. That'll be six-fifty. Departures entrance is just down there on yer left. Have a good trip and don't forget to book one of our lads again when you're back in our wee city. Our drivers have the best craic, I'll tell you that for nothing."

Ellie Rose McKee has had a number of poems and short stories published, has been blogging for over ten years, and is currently seeking representation for her debut novel. She lives in Belfast with her husband, cat, and accidental Chihuahua.

A Memoir of Eveleen Forrester
Gaynor Kane

The first of October 1911, in 23 Lendrick Street, Belfast.

Ma and I rose before the rest of the household, still in our night-clothes. She put a kettle on to boil, while I lit the fire and put the wash bowls on the table. We washed in disjointed synchronicity so that neither of us would require the towel at the same time.

Ma was so heavily pregnant that each step must have been like Everest, every time she climbed the steep staircase. The gilt frame on the mantelpiece showed a slim, handsome, young couple on their wedding day, but Ma's breasts had swollen with each baby, and her cheeks were plump now.

I woke the boys and my little sister, Mabel, the youngest of the family. She'd just started school and still needed help lacing her boots. Thin soles and uneven heels meant that those boots, previously worn by me and the boys, took all the cobbler's skill to hold them together.

Ma was in the scullery, kneading soda bread while the griddle smoked and spat. It filled the house with an aroma like heavenly manna.

'Ted pinched me!' squealed Mabel.

'Teddy, don't tease your sister.'

'What's in my piece today, Mother?' Jimmy was thirteen,

tall as a giraffe but with strong legs. His appetite could never be sated.

'Jam again, son.'

That'd be thanks to our successful blackberry-picking.

'Right, children. Hurry up! Eat breakfast quickly, or you'll be late for school,' Father's English-accented voice cut the conversation short.

'Dreamin' of your childhood, darlin'?' Ma said.

'How did you know that, Charlotte?' Father asked, with a puzzled expression.

Ma and I exchanged smiles. We seemed to be the only ones to ever detect the subtle differences in his accent. My father's family had been in shipbuilding for a least two generations, and his own father had travelled the country to different yards, building ever bigger ships. Father had adopted every local dialect. If he'd been dreaming about his adolescence, he'd have woken up speaking broad Glaswegian.

***

I knew from the moment I turned the corner coming home from work, that something was different. Our neighbours, Agnes and Molly, were standing at my door.

'Yer Ma's had the baby!' they cried.

I broke into a run, my re-soled boots pounding the street.

In my parents' bedroom, Mrs. Duncan, the midwife, was bundling up soiled bedclothes. Ma had been cleaned up, the bed had fresh linen on it, but damp curls stuck to her head, and her forehead was creased. She raised the swaddled bundle towards me, face alight with joy.

'It's a girl,' Ma said, in answer to my unspoken question. 'If Father likes it, we'll call her Winifred. Winnie.'

At bedtime, I brought the children home from my Aunt's

house in the next street. They went up in a little procession, like shepherds journeying to see Baby Jesus. I stoked up the fire and dimmed the gas lamp, then sat down across the table from Father.

'Isn't Winnie beautiful?' he said.

'She is, Father.'

'It's a wonderful day.'

'That it is.'

'Something else happened.'

'What's that, Father?'

'I got asked to go on the Titanic's maiden voyage.'

'Oh! Why?'

'They want to put together a crew to guarantee everything runs smoothly, and they've asked me to be in charge of the engines. It'll probably mean I get promoted to Foreman afterwards, with a good pay rise, too.'

'That's wonderful, Father. What an honour!' I stifled a yawn. 'Well, the excitement of the day has caught up with me. I'm exhausted, I'll check on Ma on the way to bed. Goodnight.' I knew Father didn't want a big fuss, but I couldn't help wondering how his news would change the family's fortune.

'Goodnight Eveleen dear,' he answered, as I kissed him on a weatherworn cheek.

***

On the 1st April 1912, Titanic was scheduled for sea trials

I woke early that morning. Firstly, because I hadn't slept well, due to the excitement, and secondly because the window rattled so loudly.

We went about our morning routine in awkward silence, even the wee ones. When Father was ready to leave, we lined up in front of him according to age.

'Safe travels, Father. Send us a postcard from New York.' I said, then held my breath.

'I will, Eveleen, dearest'

'I'll be the man of the house now.' Jimmy stuck his chest out as he shook Father's hand. 'I promise to look after Mother and the children while you're away, Sir.'

'You'll do a splendid job, James!'

Billy, as usual, took his lead from Jimmy. 'I'll be second in command, Sir. Don't you worry; we'll keep everything ship-shape'

'I promise not to tease Mabel,' Teddy said as he swung around and tugged Mabel's hair.

'Och, away on with ya, ya wee rascal!' Father said with a hearty laugh.

'Ouch! Silly boy!' Stepping closer to Father, Mabel threw her tiny arms around his muscular thighs. 'I'll miss you. Please can I have a seashell from the other side of the big sea?'

Father embraced Ma, pressing his cheek to hers. 'I'll miss you all so much,' he said, with eyes squeezed shut. His voice was thick, as if he had a lump in his throat.

In the corner of the room, baby Winnie wept.

***

To protect themselves against the ferocious gusts, the boys put on as many winter garments as they could while they battled alongside Father, dragging his trunk all the way to the tram.

I heard from customers in the shop that the sea trials had been cancelled due to the storm. Father returned home that night, and it was like Christmas. He spent the evening telling us stories as the wind began to diminish outside. We were all entranced, even Winnie, who'd just turned six months old. She sat gurgling and blowing bubbles, and drumming her uncoordinated hands.

The following morning, we repeated the routine of the previous day. Weather conditions were favourable for sea trials, so off my father went again. Like any other Tuesday, I went to Mr Wright's to work, stealing moments when it was quiet to read one of the books Mrs Wright lent me. She knew I had ambition and told me that times were changing.

When I returned home, my grandmother, mother and aunt were in the parlour in a circle, like some sort of coven, with little Winnie as the focus of their puckered attention. Curtains flapped in the open window, and Winnie was naked apart from her nappy. Her small body was covered in a rash, glowing like hot embers.

'Oh, thank God you're home, Eveleen. Winnie's been bawlin' all day. She's terrible ill! She's only after exhaustin' herself into a stupor!' The fear in my Mother's eyes was like a cornered animal.

'I think it's scarlet fever' announced Grandmother, shaking her head. 'Go up Templemore and fetch Doctor Morrison, dear. Hurry!'

I turned and ran.

Bringing the elderly Doctor back seemed to take forever.

'I'm afraid it's meningitis,' he said simply. 'I'll report it to the board. Pull the blind and curtains, but continue to keep the room well ventilated. Here's some chloroform, to be given at six-hourly intervals. I'll return shortly to inject her with serum. The next day or two will be critical.'

He left us reeling in shock.

Jimmy and Billy were dispatched to take word to Father at the docks. He came back with them, and announced that he was staying. I overheard him tell Ma about how his foreman had been there when the boys told him about Winnie, and how he'd automatically volunteered to go in Father's place. They saw it as a selfless act; I thought it was more about the foreman getting the glory of the maiden voyage.

Ma spent the night in the parlour, in a candlelit vigil. Mr Wright sent a block of ice down, and she religiously sponged Winnie with cold water. My father spent the entire night pacing the floorboards, praying for his baby girl.

***

Two weeks later, Winnie was much improved, her illness no longer life-threatening.

Our relief was overshadowed by the horrific news when it broke: the Titanic had struck an iceberg.

That evening, Father sat at the table, swathed in the scent of stale tobacco and whiskey. His face, covered in soot and oil from a hard day's graft on the engines, were striped by snail trails that ran from eye to jaw. He pushed his uneaten meal aside and slumped over.

'He's dead.' He pulled his fingers through his hair. 'They're *all* dead! It should have been me!' His heavy frame heaved, and a damp patch, like an oil slick, formed on the tablecloth.

We were sent to bed.

***

For weeks, it seemed, Belfast was cloaked by dense, suffocating fog. Houses had their blinds drawn in respect. Daily funerals took place for those whose bodies would probably never return to Ireland.

Father came home later and later each night. He became a shadow of his former self; no longer recognisable as the burly young man in the photograph on the fireplace. His good-natured face was shrouded by torment, which he took out on little Winifred.

90

On the first of June, I arrived home from work to find a letter on the mantelpiece, addressed to Father. At around nine-thirty, the front door was flung open and Father stumbled along the hall. He sank into a chair and Ma handed him the envelope.

Sunbury Avenue
Belfast
County Down

28th May, 1912

Mr. James Forrester
23 Lendrick Street
Belfast
County Down

My Dear Mr. Forrester,

I am writing to express my thanks to you for the tea you brought to Anthony's wake. It was very much appreciated. More importantly, I wish to tell you that I bear you no resentment. You made the right decision to remain with your family and without the benefit of foresight. Indeed no one could have predicted that the great unsinkable liner would go down on her maiden voyage. My husband went willingly in your place and was such a loyal employee of Messrs Harland and Wolff that I believe he would have made the same choice had he known the outcome of his fate.

As you know Artie was often the target of persecution by those who thought his proper name of Anthony meant he was a Catholic and he told me of your support in these incidences. I will be forever grateful to you for that. You were also very generous to let him take your trunk on the journey. I'm sure you must have lost many personal belongings. I would like to offer you some of Artie's clothes to make up for that. Please send your eldest boy to collect them.

91

I am aware that your personal circumstances have been difficult recently. I am very pleased to hear that your youngest recovered from her illness. Thanks be to God for saving her.

Yours,
Lizzie Jane

When he finished reading, he closed his eyes, swallowed, and bowed his head. Gently, Mother took the letter.

'See. Didn't I tell you? Nobody thinks it's your fault, not even *that* poor woman!'

'But Charlotte!'' He beat a fist against his protruding breast-bone. 'In here, it feels like my fault. And in here.' He knocked on his skull with the same fist. 'In here, the voices are telling me it's my fault!'

'Eveleen. Check the weans for us, dear,' Ma said.

I closed the door behind me, but pressed my ear to the wood.

'Look, Jim, dearest,' Ma said. 'I don't mean to be callous, but it's time for some plain speakin'. If you carry on the way you're goin' you might as well have gone to sea and not come back. Now! You just pull yourself together, for this family needs a man.'

Gaynor Kane, East Belfast born and bred, wrote this memoir inspired by family folklore – James Forrester was her great-grandfather. Gaynor's debut poetry collection is due to be released in 2020, and she is author of *Memory Forest*, published by Hedgehog Poetry Press. Follow her at Twitter @gaynorkane and www.gaynorkane.com.

Dear Rowan
Rosie Burrows

Belfast, 26th April 2020.

To my grandson, 9 months, and all our children.

Dear Rowan,

I listen to the song of sparrows on the magnolia tree, as the Scots Pine dances in the jazzy breeze.

I put two eggs into a cast iron pot and turn them to simmer. Gently. It's peaceful, like a pre-60's childhood day. A long day without speeding cars and perpetual planes.

Now, and for the last month, those of us not working on the frontlines are sheltered at home in Belfast, rarely going out except for essential items and exercise.

Spaced two metres from each other.

I am separated from you by sixty miles, and I think of you up in Ballycastle, looking directly out to Rathlin Island and Fair Head, with the Mull of Kintyre hazy in the distance — like the song says.

'*Mull of Kintyre, oh mist rolling in from the sea…*"

We've been blessed lately with clear skies, *Lovely Day*. That's what Bill Withers would have said.

Just one look at you and I know it's gonna be a lovely day.

Bill Withers —a singer who passed over on a lovely day a

few weeks ago.

I'm going to play *Lovely Day, Lean On Me* and *Ain't No Sunshine When You're Gone* for you on the *Pauer*, our old piano. Grandpap and Nana O'Connor won it at the Holy Family parish ballot; they had a choice of an unwanted piano or a bottle of Bushmills, and they chose the piano.

We'll turn on Spotify and dance to celebrate when *I take one look at you.* You up on your pegs, me your helper.

I'll take you into town to the Oh Yeah Music Centre in the old whiskey distillery on Gordon Street, and we'll sing a '78 by Jilted John. *Gordon's not a moron.* I can't wait to tell you, when you're the age of *'Teenage dreams so hard to beat,'* about the energetic and creative inclusive space for young people of punk, ska, soul, trad, reggae, folk, alternative-dance scene in Belfast at the Harp, Pound, Orpheus, Delta, Crescent and Warehouse.

Shake it up baby! Dance and shout.

There are rainbows in the front windows of homes here on the Ormeau Road; messages to NHS workers, frontliners and those respecting the two-metre distance. The same messages are yarn-bombed on tree-lined streets, children blow bubbles and play games in avenues lined by motionless cars. Anxieties about an airborne virus run deep, but we breathe deep in this pollution-free atmosphere.

Elders hang out in the sun, on front patios and green patches, chatting to passers-by who pause, eager for craic and conversation. Nervous systems have been reset; time, space and community support regulate the natural grief-cycle. We feel our way through shock, denial, anger, sadness, acceptance — meaning-making in the profession of Mamo Rosie.

The meaning I make is that these are evolutionary moments: feedback loops, painful raps — full of tragedy and suffering — telling us to back the feck off wild spaces and creatures, and stop exploiting other human beings, before it's too late.

I hear Aretha Franklin, singing *Respect*, in stereo. And, you and me, babe, will dance to that, too, when we finally reconnect.

I accept the data, the IPCC report that says we have until 2030 — not 2050 — to turn around the damage to the earth. You'll be ten in 2030, Rowan. We will listen and act wisely to protect the foundations of our wellbeing. No point in cynicism and complacency; complaining and polarising. We adults need a growth spurt in maturity.

Storytellers are rising from our hearths.

Once upon a time, in a city called Belfast, a diverse tribe of rainbow writers, members of Women Aloud NI, bore witness, offering omens —portals into possibilities, reigniting imaginations grown weary and numb from the same old, same old. We gathered at the Big Fish by the River Lagan, a powerful Salmon of Wisdom sculpture in ceramic blue and white. We sounded our good vibrations, sensations, colours, smells, tastes, feelings, footprints into the future. Stories, poems, handwritten letters. *One people.*

Dear Rowan, the science on climate change, on pandemics, on suicide, on other social and ecological preventables is clear. Prime Minister Jacinda Ardhern, in New Zealand, and others, right now, are effectively minimising tragedy, other leaders are not. We are experiencing in our hearts and hands what the eco-writer Joanna Macy, calls the 'great turning' — the shift from the Industrial Growth Society to a life-sustaining civilization.

Pachamama, the Earth Mother of the Incas, will survive no matter what. She's stretching out a hand, with stings in air and wing, inviting and guiding us to a different dance.

We have the technology to tune into a new rhythm and rhyme that can set all of us free, enabling us to be who we really are.

On a quiet day like today, I listen to the song of sparrows on the magnolia tree as the Scots Pine dances in the jazzy breeze. Can you feel the presence of *Pachamama?* Can you hear her singing our selkie soul-skins homewards?

Her Children-of-Lir swans, rising on the coldest sea of Moyle, hearing words as waves and particles; as male and female and between?

Art can contribute to evolving us and our world.

Love and limits,

Mamo Rosie

Rosie Burrows has worked as a trauma/loss and resilience specialist, in Northern Ireland and internationally. Her published writing since 1986 explores and supports personal and collective evolution, including our central human need to be compassionate witnesses to our own and others' creative and suffering voice. Follow her at www.rosieburrows.com.

A Victim No More
Alison Black

A victim no more,
Being a victim is a casualty of grief,
Be a survivor of the universe,
Be a positive spark of light.

Be an inspiration to other people,
Survival of the fittest,
Be on the right track to recovery,
Don't be weak but strong,
Open your heart to people.

Alison Black is a writer from Belfast, who has been writing for ten years. Alison writes from the heart and has been lucky to have had poems published. She writes about true life, not fiction.

County Derry/Londonderry

The north west boasts no less a bounty of talented women writers. **Anne McMaster's** *poem, Hunger, is followed by* **Mel Bradley's** *love letter to her hometown, which reflects the cultural hub the city is in all its glory and beauty.*

*   **Sue Divin's** *trip to the dentist might have you squirming, while* **Anne McMaster's** *second poem, Silver, heralds the beauty in the rural environs of the maiden city.* **Elizabeth McQuillan's** *short story is steeped in themes of faith and finally,* **Kerriann Speers** *gives us a lyrical and moving conversation with her Grandmother that encapsulates Northern Irish conversations to a tee.*

Hunger
Anne McMaster

Heads pressed low like cattle walking into rain,
we ploughed into the bleak November dusk -
following our father as he strode into the dark.
The cattle that he checked each winter's night
moved slowly through a sloping, generous field
once full of rich, thick grass -
a bowl for a still, hot summer sun -
that now lay scuffed and bare as it emptied with the year.
Winds whistled through desolate hedges;
hulking low and beast-like
in the darkest corners of the field before lifting to the sky.
We knew this sound for what it was - had grown with it -
but we remained aloof, buckling down our fear
like strapping a satchel closed on an unwelcome task.
It was the phone lines -
taut as webbing in that bitter, threatening sky -
that caught our imaginations then set all scrambling free
like mindless, scuttering frenzied things.
Plucked by a prowling breeze, the lines began to hum;
a chorus of howling voices carried within the wind
seemed to echo the approach of some unholy things.

This was the voice of lost and lonely souls
caught high in the web of night;
a ravenous legion that capered madly above,
seeking to fall upon us and then take their fill.
We recognised the sounds of hunger - and we ran.
I remember turning from my father in that night-time field
to race, dry-mouthed, in pistoning, thick, fat steps for home;
the heavy rubber of my muddied boots
slapping against my calves as I shrieked and ran.
Three small girls raced each other to outrun the siren song.
We ran towards the light, towards safety,
towards what we knew.
The night closed fast and low behind us -
hungry, dark, unfed.

Anne McMaster lives on an old farm in rural mid-Ulster. After a
lengthy career as a lecturer, playwright and theatre director, she now
works as a professional voice actor, editor and poet. Her work has been
published extensively in the USA, Canada, the UK and Ireland.

Derry
Mel Bradley

If stones could speak and walls could breathe
if the streets could sing to us their prayer
the ancient trees that murmur softly
and the river whispered stories to the air
What would this city, my home, tell you?
What tales of fancy would it share?
Derry, my birthplace, a city like no other
with more names than one place could ever bear
a border town with cityscape dreams
divided by more than its river, a narrative unlike elsewhere.

A story that is steeped in conflicting traditions
of factory girls, apprentice boys and dance hall beats
A civil rights movement that demanded better days
68's outcry of disobedience, people took to these streets
The following year and some defiant graffiti
a pub conversation and a young man's upbeat
declaration sets in motion recognition
that speaks out in iconic rhythmic heartbeats
Now a symbol the world over of hope against
adversity, injustice and societal mistreats.

400 years, the city grew up around those walls
crippling unemployment and the Derry dads' fame
Music became our tribal call in troubled times
The working class soul and punk's rebellious flame
spoke truths of dissatisfied and angry youths
loudly in brash tones that relinquished any shame
Derry, there's music in the water and the air
It's our lifeblood, our nourishment and claim
The steady sounds of the factory machines
kept this city flowing in perfect metronomic frame.

I fell in love with you when I was eight
a child enamoured with your dynamic flare
All Hallows Eve and the streets were electric
devils danced with angels devoid of care

The night was kissed with music and laughter
as the crowds gathered in Guildhall Square
The veil had thinned and demons sinned
and men walked around in skirts, legs bare
Grown adults free to play dress up and pretend
Mischief and mayhem their prescribed pair

I marvelled at the costumes and creativity
this city's people chose to wear
For one night, despite the normal stresses
we shed off that cloak of utter despair
we fill the streets with joy and excitement
care-free childlike pleasure our only dare

From that beautiful night, now some thirty years on
I haven't lost the spark of that love affair
I keep its embers burning vibrant
And hope that we will always share
in this paganistic ritual of honouring
our ancestors, the pageantry and fare

We huddle together on the banks of the Foyle
to watch, as fireworks light up the night
Derry, my birthplace, my city, my darling
your beauty and colour, breathtakingly bright
Once called a city of culture we celebrated
and waited for the luminous global spotlight
Quickly turned missed opportunity to showcase
leaving a bitter taste of things that were not quite
It's true we had a year of spectacle and wonder
and diminished funding, again became our plight

We sit on the boundary edges of this country
a mere stone's throw from our Donegal kin
Political uncertainty in a dithering government
an economic vacuum and industry thin
Identity issues and border-crossing fears
power-sharing leadership that won't give in
Corruption, scandals and a language stalemate
Meanwhile our city strategy needs rescued from the bin
On shaky ground lies our peace agreement
and we're just expected to take it all on the chin.

Now, don't get me wrong, my darling city, Derry,
you'll always be the place I call home and call heart
because of the people, a vibrant community
that at its core values its craft and its art
We come together when we need to
each person, always eager, to take on their part
You see it clearly in our festivals and celebrations,
in our music and poetry that was there from the start
Our hospitable welcome to strangers as friends
this familial embrace is what sets us apart

If stones could speak and walls could breathe
if the streets could sing to us their prayer
the ancient trees that murmur softly
and the river whispered stories to the air
Where would this city's story take you?
What adventures would you find hidden there?

Mel Bradley is a spoken word artist/poet, writer, burlesque per-
former, multimedia artist, actor and creative genius, with the attention
span of a gnat. An ACNI-supported, queer feminist artist, she has per-
formed at the Bogside Inn, the Royal Albert Hall, Open House,
Edinburgh Fringe and Paris Lit Up.

Away with The Fairies
Sue Divin

Cian slouched in the dentist's waiting room. He jiggled a stone and a chewing gum wrapper in his pocket. Was the tooth-fairy real? If she was, would the dentist explain why he always got 5p when Rory Donnelly got two quid?

Fair enough, there was the odd day, or three, he chewed a polo-mint to dupe his Ma about minding to clean his teeth, and Rory Donnelly had a swanky electric batman toothbrush, but two quid? That was five Mars bars of difference, if you got the multi-packs, and those tasted lethal if you ate three in a row behind the shed. Four and you'd be sick. This, he knew from experience.

But was the dentist like confession? Was one wiggly black tooth a sin?

'Noreen Hughes,' the receptionist announced. No one budged. Cian stretched his toes as he swung his legs under the plastic chair. They almost reached the floor.

'Mrs. Noreen. Hughes.'

The wrinkly lady in the corner lifted her white stick and bag. 'I'm near blind,' she said. 'Not deaf.'

Cian minded doing his first confession in the Longtower Chapel last year. Yet another time Rory Donnelly had milked it, compared to him. The way it worked was you got scrubbed to the nineties, even your ears, and everyone at break practiced making up the wee sins and forgetting the big ones.

'Get your game face on,' Kelly Devine had toul' him, all expert. 'Let on you lied three times to your Ma and cursed once, maybe twice. It's only one Hail Mary for a curse or lie.'

She *knew* stuff, that Kelly, even about kissing, for she had three older sisters already at St.Cecilia's big-school. It wasn't fair. Cian narrowed his eyes. When you were the oldest, you were stuck with doing all the finding-out for yourself *and* always being told 'Grow up, would ye?'

No-one ever explained that the pressure of being nearly nine was worse than the seven-times-tables.

He should've asked Kelly about the dentist. Harry Meenan swore the dentist had a rocket chair and Avengers stickers, but then again, Harry Meenan had bust his head in a crash-landing off Bull Park climbing frame when he was seven-and-a-half, and he had the thing that made words dance on the page. Apparently, it wasn't as fun as it sounded.

The tooth was no fun either. It hurt. Cian rubbed his jaw and glanced out the wee squares on the window to where Da was still smoking a roll-up on Abercorn Road, and nattering on the mobile. He'd meant to ask Da about what Rory said about the pink stuff. '*Never, ever swallow it or your insides melt to jelly. You die in a puddle.*' His nod had been extra serious. Cian shifted in the chair. It couldn't be true, could it? Then again, Da was pure scared of the dentist and Das weren't meant to be scared of anything.

'You've got to take him,' he'd heard Ma say through the bedroom floor. 'Sure am't I working?'

Da had mumbled something back that might've been a smart-arse comment, for the kitchen went quiet and the back door slammed.

108

A baldy man walked back into the waiting room. His face looked weird on one side. Cian's eyes widened.

'Do you pay for your treatment, Mr Carlin?'

There was pink dribble at the man's mouth. The way he slurred 'Aye' sounded like Da late on a Saturday.

'Mouth frozen?' asked the receptionist.

Cian curled his ankles tight round the chair legs and sat bolt upright. Mr Carlin's voice was melting '...drillin'... injayshun...'

Da was back. 'You're white as toothpaste, wee man,' he said.

'Cian Doherty?' The receptionist smiled.

***

'Do you brush your teeth every day?' asked the dentist, through a blue Darth-Vader thing.

'Aye.' *One Hail Mary*. Cian gripped the sides of the chair. It *was* a rocket chair, except it was beige. Proper rocket chairs were black or silver.

'Twice a day?

'Eh... Mostly.' Cian eyed Da. *Two Hail Marys*. Da looked edgy. The rocket chair whirred as it tilted back, then up. Through the dark glasses the nurse had put on him, Cian squinted sideways. Holy Jesus. *Three Hail Marys*. The dentist was clinking metal tools – grim reaper Hallowe'en stuff, only without fake blood. Cian dug his nails into the beige plastic. What if Rory wasn't winding him?

'Lucky it's a wiggly milk tooth's gone rotten. I'll take it out now. Be sure and scrub those other teeth, Cian, won't you? Fairies might only leave a pound for a bad tooth you know. Open wide.'

One pound? For a black tooth? Cian went to speak but the words didn't come. Instead, his mouth went dry, and every

109

muscle in his body stretched tight as he stared at Darth Vader's fingers hovering over a weapon. Cian blinked as the gadget buzzed. Screwing his eyes shut, he braced himself as the scrapy thing attacked his mouth. *Owwww*. Clink. The cold of a new tool and a tug at his jaw. He winced, eyes shooting open and fixing on a bloody black and white nugget in the tweezers at the end of his nose. He jolted upright and the room spun.

'Take a wee sip,' said the nurse.

Cian glugged. It smelled like the William Street swimming baths.

'Spit here.'

Spit? The world swam has he considered the empty glass and watched the pink froth of his dribble slide in the white basin.

'You didn't swallow it, did you?'

Oh God. Oh God. Oh God. Rory was right. Cian's stomach churned, his head light as he watched his feet blur. He'd never even liked jelly...

***

There were low voices. Cian became aware of the breeze drifting in from a window. He blinked. The blur of faces began to refocus. The dentist, Da and the receptionist. All staring.

'You were away with the fairies there a minute,' smiled Da.

Cian looked at his feet. No pink jelly. Anywhere. Instead, a shiny pound coin had magicked itself onto his lap.

***

He held his head high as he strutted through the Bogside, the pound clasped tight in his fist, Captain America, Iron Man and Hulk stuck onto his school jumper. Running his tongue round his teeth, he found the gap, then counted on. Three things were now sure. First, fairies were real; second, Harry Meenan was for getting a Mars bar tomorrow and third, if he could

110

find the permanent black marker Ma hid after the wallpaper incident, there was at least another three quid's worth of wigglable teeth ready to trade.

Sue Divin is a Derry based writer, originally from Armagh. She gives thanks daily to ACNI for her SIAP award and concedes only under duress and/or alcoholic influence to having work published in a range of literary journals. Her début novel, *Guard Your Heart*, will be published in 2021 by Macmillan.

Silver
Anne McMaster

These roads were horse tracks once;
curving slowly into the rising hill,
easing the passage of harvest-heavy carts hauled
by teams of horses to the waiting farms.
Huge, stolid beasts - their sweating heads held low,
necks taut, while their hooves spat sounds - ice-sharp –
into the darkening sky.
I'm told that highwaymen roamed here too;
their cache still buried in the fields above the farm.
So when I walk these shadowed roads in winter
and the moon is all I have,
my thoughts are now of silver:
the cool wash of moonlight across a sour and empty hedge,
wild eyes gleaming, wet with fear,
at a sudden dark interruption.
The glint of silver at a horse's foaming mouth.

Lord of the Land
Elizabeth McQuillan

The first that they knew of him was when the waters whispered his name as they flowed down from the hills to the seas. *He'll come back*, they whispered, as they rippled over the rocks of their stony beds. *He'll come back, and is slowly making his way through all the land that he once ruled.* They bubbled with excitement to think that maybe, just maybe, things would go back to the way they were. At the estuary, the ocean opened up and swallowed the churning white water, drowning the excitement, tempering the joy. It would wait and see, as it always did. But still the waters spoke his name.

The wind sang a song of welcome as it blew over the land, sending leaves to dancing, and grass to rippling like the waters of the ocean. It tugged at the coats of the people as they walked below, and cheekily stole a few hats, adding their rise and fall to its song. It ruffled the surface of the water. It blew around him as he walked his familiar path, whispering all the rumours and stories it had picked up as it blew about the county.

The sun watched, as it always did. Distant in time, and in space, it merely sent out its rays in the hope that somewhere out there, someone would find sustenance from them.

Earth felt his footfalls upon it, and flowers grew up in his wake, blooming in profusion and releasing their scent to dance on the wind. Trees stirred in their old groves, deep and forgotten roots uncoiling as they woke up from their long slumber. Long limbs twisted in their silent language as the stories started to be told again.

He had returned.

And he smiled to himself as the world awoke around him. He had stepped through the fog into a world of concrete and glass. Stunted trees grew in silence with shortened roots, their lilting voices silenced. The Earth was quiet under its solid covering, and only a few hardy weeds poked through where they could. Water flowed through the drains and the sewers, and it alone felt his arrival.

Only the quiet sun shone down as it always had.

Everything had changed, since he'd last walked through these lands. All around him humans walked, unknowing and uncaring of the world that turned around them. Their eyes passed over him as they looked through him. He bent down and touched the feathery leaves of moss that stubbornly grew through the slabs that surrounded him. He felt the little spark flare up in utter pleasure, as roots sank deeper. Around it, concrete cracked.

He smiled and moved on.

He walked from the centre of the town, feeling the little moss stretching out, passing along its energy to other patches that lined the streets. The earth felt the touch of his energy and he felt the living spark start to rise. Over the river, two bridges stretched, one cluttered with twisted metal and burning fire, the other a pathway for humans. Below them, the river flowed, smooth and deep.

He whispered his name, felt the wind catch it as it left his lips, and saw the whirlpools in the river flare to life, spinning in silent delight. The ocean tide, deep and slow, acknowledged him, but returned to serious contemplation. On the far bank, grass and trees called to him, begging for his touch.

There was no way that he could not listen to them. His fingers reached out to caress leaf and branch, even as his bare feet lightly passed over the grass. He felt life renew, bright and bold, growing tall, strong and proud. He tilted his head to the skies, and listened to the wind.

He walked.

Where once he had ruled, now humans ruled. Where once trees and grass grew and murmured, structures of stone and glass now rose. But underneath it all, the earth was still strong. And in some places, green still ruled.

The forests and woodlands still towered over the land, their roots sunk deep into the world. Fields whispered their promise of golden harvests and fat cattle, sun ripened grass and fleecy sheep. It spoke of the care of those with earth-stained hands, of their stewardship and of their friendship. And under all, their love.

And he smiled again.

Under everything, under the concrete and the glass and the humans running around like ants, there was still love. Beneath the green, under the elements that bound the world together, there was still love.

And with that love, he was content. This place no longer needed his rule; the land welcomed him but did not need him. For all their faults, while the world held fast to the singular truth, he could rest happy.

He whispered his farewell to the wind, hearing it take up the song in a mournful key, setting the leaves on the trees to weeping. The trees reminded themselves of other stories of his coming and his going and his promise to always be with them.

As the fog rose and swallowed him again, carrying him back into his rest, he reached out once more with a thrum of power, one last blessing for the county of his heart.

Born in England, raised in Scotland and now living in Northern Ireland with her husband and a space-mad child, **Elizabeth McQuillan** has dabbled her toes into the waters of self-publishing. She also has a short story published in the *Alien Days* anthology by Castrum Press.

At Your Grandmother's Table
Kerriann Speers

As the early half-light gently wakens Slieve Gallion,
She'll watch the pink rose bush your grandfather planted.
The blousy blossoms unfurling a perfect sun salutation
As she rinses her two best mugs.
You'll say "Let the dishwasher get those."
And she'll say "Sure there's no point, now I'm on my own."
She'll bypass the fancy coffee maker.
She'll give you instant coffee, two heaped teaspoonfuls,
Because you like it strong. Straight from the kettle.
She'll wear the blue jumper because you bought it.
"That Christmas, do you remember?"
She'd look like the Virgin Mary,
If she were allowed to grow old.
And at your grandmother's table,
She'll ask "How was school?
How was work? How are the kids?"
And you'll say "Fine, fine, fine."
But she knows it's not and the words will tumble out
On to the plastic-backed tablecloth.
And she will say,
       "You think that's bad, wait till you hear this…"

And she will tell you about a relative
    you don't remember meeting,
Whose husband has died or who has cancer or
    who has lost their job.
And you're supposed to feel better. And you do.
Not because of the story. Because of the voice.
And she won't say I love you
She'll say "I got that cake you like."
And she will tell you about your mother
When she was your age. The tricks she got up to.
Then she'll tell you about the day you were born,
Like it was yesterday. Because it was, to her.
And she was there. The first to hold you.
And she'll say "I was premature, you know.'
And you do, but you listen anyway
To the story of the baby.
Born too soon. Shoebox for a cot.
No eyelashes, no nails.
Not meant to live.
But she's here, at the table.
Dressed in that blue jumper,
You bought it; do you remember?

Kerriann Speers is a fiction writer and occasional poet, published in Writing Magazine and the Bangor Literary Journal. Living along the North Coast of Ireland, Kerriann is a member of Flowerfield Writers Group, Portstewart. An early school report read, "Kerriann reads words that aren't necessarily on the page." This remains true.

County Down

*County Down has provided us with many talented writers. We open with a beautiful poem by **Amy Louise Wyatt**, followed immediately by another poem, this one created by **Grainne Tobin**. Next, we have a piece of writing told from the point of view of a drumlin, from the imagination of **Kerry Buchanan**, who is one of the two editors of the anthology.*

*   **Caroline Johnstone** brings us a beautiful haibun that speaks of a happy childhood in County Down, and **Lesley Walsh**, the second joint editor of the anthology, gives us a tale inspired by the current Coronavirus crisis.*

*   **Mairead Breen** has given us a lovely poem, followed by a short story on a similar theme by **Florence Heyhoe**. A beautiful piece by **Karen Mooney**, inspired by Mount Stewart, is followed by Home Truths, a poem by **Kelly Creighton**, giving us a glimpse back into the past, where she grew up in Bangor. Homecoming, by **Rosemary Tumilty** does the same for Kilkeel.*

*   Finally, we have Greyabbey, a poem by **Meg McCleery** and then this chapter finishes with a piece of memoir by **Paula Ryder** that tells of her childhood in Crossgar.*

The Seals at Ballykinlar
Gráinne Tobin

When a helicopter buzzes low, they barely blink —
a hundred and eighty-five seals laid out on the beach,
sunbathing under the military firing range.
A man tries our telescope and says, *They're like us!*
They're here so quietly, I thought they were rocks.

Tidy harbour seals slide out of the sea, glossy
as mussel shells or liquorice, streaming saltwater
from their synchronised-swimming in black satin,
but then flub along the sand in a hopping motion
that never gets off the ground and looks a little shameful,
the frictionless life gone frumpy and gritty on land,
though they move fast, ditching style for function,
shuffling their way to spread imaginary towels
and present soaking pelts to the sun.

A month before the pups are due, these greys lie back,
holding flippers open in the warm air, damp mounds
of belly fluffing to pale fur, not sleek and mermaidy

but heavy, turning over like slack rolls of carpet,
rearranging their sort-of-hands for balance,
all supervised by a big whiskery grey,
the beachmaster who keeps himself apart.

You have to get near to hear them singing.

Gráinne Tobin lives in Newcastle, Co Down. Her books are *Banjaxed*,
The Nervous Flyer's Companion and *The Uses of Silk*. She has poems in
magazines, anthologies and online in *Poethead*, the Poetry Ireland ar-
chive and the *Troubles* archive of the Arts Council of Northern Ireland.

Beannchar
Amy Louise Wyatt

From the lean in Abbey Street your rigid
spire's seen tangled in a knot of trees;
yet six feet on you are a free-beaked bird
now set to rocket lofty heights. Close-up,

Saint Malachy's wall unrests, unbuilds itself
in the replay of time; allows me but a peek
of what will one day pierce the clouds
and burst the sacks of rain upon our heads.

Beannchar, tell me that it's true, that monks
once lived and died upon your land,
and buried in the ground below my feet
lie bones of scribes and holy men.

I wonder if it's hard to rest beneath the steps
of children you sent forth into Vallis Angelorum?

Amy Louise Wyatt is a poet from Bangor. She was shortlisted for the Seamus Heaney Award in 2018 and 2020 and won the 2019 Poetrygram Prize. She is Editor of The Bangor Literary Journal. Amy's debut pamphlet *'A Language I Understand'* is forthcoming in 2020 with Indigo Dreams.

The Drumlin's* Tale
Kerry Buchanan

Eggs laid in baskets
From an ice sheet's frozen womb.
The songs they could sing!

Once, I was one; then I was many; now I am one.

An irresistible force wrenched me from my bedrock, carrying me within its frozen maw. It jostled and crushed me against others, scraping and chipping at my raw edges as the ice rolled us about.

In time, the ice became thinner. Meltwater trickled down through cracks, warming the glacier and opening fissures. One day, a beam of light stabbed deep into my hiding place, melting the ice beneath me so I tumbled towards the ground.

My flinty heart sang. I would find my bedrock again, settle back into the scar of my separation and fuse once more with Mother Earth.

I was not alone in my belief. All around me, smaller boulders clattered together in a loose herd, excited by the sense of a journey nearly ended. Together, we bounced across the ground, adding to our number. When my forward movement was arrested by a seam of granite, they all piled up behind me, pinned to my back by the force of the still-crawling ice sheet.

We lay there for so very long, while the ice went on without us. I called out to my bedrock, seeking its familiar vibrations, but there was no reply. Ice turned to water, glacier to puddles. I held firm, protecting the myriad boulders that pressed against me for comfort, and together we waited.

Seasons changed.

Aeons passed.

Mother Earth took pity on us. She cast a blanket of her own skin over us, binding us ever closer together. Our blanket thickened, shaped by wind and water until we became a smooth oval, a community thrown together by fate. Trees sent their roots delving between us, forming a web of communication with the outside world.

Through their leaves and branches, we heard news of life returning: birds that carried seeds and insects; hare and stoat and light-footed deer. Gradually, the world above reshaped itself into a green and busy land.

A new species walked there. They hunted and gathered and lived in balance with Mother Earth. They nurtured their young and honoured their old ones, working together for the benefit of all. We welcomed their feet upon our turf, even when they felled our trees and turned them into spitting orange scars in our surface. The chatter of their young was like music, reminding us of meltwater trickling past us in times past, but they became so numerous that even that sound began to sicken us.

Their mouths became ever hungrier until our trees were massacred in numbers that could not be replaced. The surface of our mound became arid, the grass parched. The pools of water in the hollows between us and the mounds around us, once teeming with life, became still and silent, reeking of death and putrefaction.

And still the two-legs came, digging deep into our skin to build their shelters. They smashed bedrock, ripping from it the arteries that made us whole, that held us together. They covered huge expanses of Mother Earth with their own ugly mimicry of veins: long, stinking lines and squares of black and white that prevented the rain from sinking into the earth.

Even when the floods came, they did not learn.

Even when Mother Earth shook and trembled in pain and fear, they did not learn.

Even when the rivers dried up and the ice caps melted, they did not learn.

There is silence, now, in the air above us. The few surviving trees, twisted, deformed shadows of their ancestral forms, still whisper to us. The news they tell is of two-legs dying. They fight and raid each other's food stores. Instead of nurturing their old ones, they deprive them of the means to live and abandon them to die, lonely and alone.

Above our own mound, we no longer hear the patter of the two-legs' feet. No foul-smelling metal boxes speed along the black veins. No shrill voices chatter and laugh. No machines rip deep into Mother Earth.

All is silent.

Except the birdsong. That is growing ever more beautiful.

Now, our lakes are alive with fish and larvae, and fleet-footed deer roam, grazing in fields that are filled with wildflowers. They are hunted by packs of wild hunters, but not the two-legs. Bees are returning, no longer poisoned.

Insects feed on the decomposing corpses of two-legs, growing fat and multiplying. They become organised, harvesting the fruits of trees and bushes, setting up a pollination programme for beneficial plants, building communities that work together for the advantage of all.

Mother Earth is sinking back into a pleasant slumber, allowing her children to live in peace. Here in our drumlin, we settle a little more deeply, enjoying the sun on our turf once more.

But what is that noise?

The ants delve deep. They excavate the boulders that make up our whole, chipping away until they overwhelm us with sheer numbers. We do not need the trees to tell us that they are building now, using stone instead of earth for their homes. Wasps are changing their habits. These days they eat living wood, and their numbers are so unimaginably great that the trees cannot reproduce fast enough to match their voracious appetites.

How can they not see?

How can they not remember?

How can they not learn from the two-legs' suicidal errors?

The ants are here now, injecting some caustic liquid into the fissures in my surface, breaking apart my body.

It burns.

It liquifies me, dissolving knowledge accumulated over hundreds and thousands of seasons.

It is time to say goodbye, while I still—

*Drumlins are post-glacial hills, shaped like upturned spoons. From above, they resemble a basket of eggs, and are a well-known feature of the County Down landscape.

Kerry Buchanan is a retired vet, now full-time carer, who wrote her first novel in 2014. She has had short stories published both online and in print and has occasionally been lucky enough to win prizes – and the competitions weren't even fixed. She writes science fiction, fantasy, and crime. Follow her at www.kerrybuchanan.co.uk.

Desire Lines
Caroline Johnstone

Sun baked, we poked round the edges of the Big House lake,
spearing fish we never caught. Heading home, we heard faint
    laughter,
left the beaten track. Through the hush hush of deep
    summer woods
we discovered the garden, stopped at the edge, observing.

rhododendrons drop white petals
alternate green stripes
perfect lawn interrupted

Big doors opened up a life beyond the front hall we would
    stand in, hoping
to research something for a school project. Adults lounged
    on easy chairs
under blue parasols, shaded by dark oaks and monkey puzzle
    trees
in an idleness we did not recognise but envied.

children's soft cotton dresses
coloured balls whacked through hoops
storybook picture.

Invited forward like children at sweet shop windows we
        drank this in with
cherry red juice in Wimbledon glasses, thwacked our way
        round the course,
not noticing they'd all gone in from the heat and the
        inconvenience
of uninvited guests in mismatched clothes, cheap wellies.

no storeroom no barn
rooks search for roosts
soft lining longing

Caroline Johnstone grew up in Co Down and now lives by the sea on the west coast of Scotland. Author of books daring people to be happier, her poems have been published in the UK, Ireland and the U.S. Her first collection will be published by Red Squirrel Press in 2021.

Georgie in Stockings
Lesley Walsh

1975

Ma handed me the spoon, straight from the bowl, thick with butter-coloured cream. 'Here you go,' she said. 'Don't be spilling anything down yourself now, Georgie – Father will be home soon.'

It was so sweet and comforting on my tongue. I tried not to spill it down myself, but a little dollop dropped from the spoon on to my sweater. Ma gave me that look that made me want to pee, and her face turned red. She reached for the tea towel and wet a corner, twisting it as her eyes narrowed. But then Father's home-time noise was at the front door, and she set the tea towel down behind her so he couldn't see it. He didn't allow such things.

Father whooshed open the door and I dropped the wooden spoon as I ran to him. He picked me up, hugging me tight. I smelled the smell he brought home from work every day and my heart felt bigger in my chest. The smell came off the black from work - the stuff that looked like the flour Ma and I made into cakes, only the bits dusted across his face, were bigger. I didn't mind it when it rubbed on to me when I pushed my nose into his neck, all bristly and rough, because under the black flour smell, I smelled Father. It was his smell; the one he had since I could remember. Ma always told him to wash it from his face and hands before tea, but I wished he could wear it all evening, for it made him look like the Vikings and heroes he told me about in his tales at bedtime.

1990

When Ma went next door, I ran to the window and looked out, beyond the dark, green-black of the hillside and down to the town. I threw a glance back at the door and listened. It was quiet. I tiptoed to the old Singer that Ma's Ma had used and fished out the weathered leather case tucked underneath. Inside were the binoculars Father had brought home years ago, the ones he said would bring the outside world to us when we couldn't get down to it. I loved them best at night-time, when the people below burned a thousand lights, from the shops and the cursed places with the drink that Ma didn't let Father visit.

Ma didn't like me using the binoculars, now Father was gone. If she caught me with them, she'd hiss words like "corrupt" and "damnation" out of the side of her mouth, like old Mrs. Browne three doors up, when she spat the horrible black chaw from her toothless bake.

Father had come up the hill to join Ma when he was 20, just like me now, and he'd stayed up here all these years, though he worked down the town the odd time.

He used to take me down there when I was small enough for him to tuck me under his arm. He did it when Ma was doing a fitting for one of the ladies, and he'd say, 'Come on Georgie, let's go down the town.'

But she'd turn red in the face when we got home. She'd fire words at us like sharp little bullets, so we didn't get going half as much as I'd have liked. Down the town there'd be pink rock that I'd lick and suck, and it'd be sharp between my little teeth, then gratifyingly crumbly. Father would say, 'Sure, if they rot, you'll get bigger ones soon, but don't tell Ma.'

I hadn't been down the town since the days of Father, but I ached to sneak into the dark, green-black of the night, and observe the life under the lights, and watch the people who weren't old like Ma and the ladies. To see another man like Father, or any other man or woman. There was only one other man after Father, but he left the cottages about ten years ago. I don't know if he left on foot or in a coffin. Ma said she was glad when it was just us left, with only the ladies, so I daren't ask her why or how he left.

I peered through the eyeglasses that brought the town right up to the end of my nose and saw the cars I used to see with Father. They drove up and down the long strip, close to the edge of the sea, before they disappeared to some place I've never been, round the coast. I'd love to ride in one of those cars with people like me, and hear what they talked about, and see where it was they were going when they disappeared round the coast.

I saw the spot where all the car lights stopped and merged, like the cluster of the Seven Sisters that Father always pointed out to me in the skies above our wee line of cottages.

I always wished I had six sisters or brothers, or a mixture of both, so I wouldn't have Ma all to myself, without Father here to tell me tales at bedtime, and tuck me under his arm, and buy me pink rock.

2020
Ma suggested that the next time I should shave my legs, so the black hairs wouldn't show through the stockings.

'I'll show you how to shave, and you'll never know you ever had them. The ugly old hairs, I mean – you don't want them showing through. Silly of me, wasn't it, not thinking of it before? But I wonder if any of the ladies even shave their own legs anymore. Probably haven't for years.'

'Okay Ma,' I said. I went over the bed and sat down and looked at the hairs through the stockings. I began to take them off, gently, so they wouldn't run, just like she'd shown me. The hairs were really noticeable. Long black curls flattened under the ancient, diaphanous fabric, that sprang up as I peeled the stockings down to my toes.

"And for God's sake, make sure the fasteners are secure next time," Ma said.

"Yes, Ma." I ran the stockings through my fingers. Amazingly well-preserved, for the age of them. They'd been Ma's when she was a young woman.

"Come now, for your tea, Georgie. While it's hot," she called from the kitchen.

"It's okay, Ma. I'm not feeling very well. I'll just get into bed," I told her.

"You're sick? You never said. You should have said, with me beside you all night and you not saying! You better not pass it on to me!" she shouted. "You're off walking that dog and not telling me where it is you go; you could catch it and give it to me. What if I catch my death and you're left here all on your own?" She was breathless by the end of her rant.

"I've not been anywhere but Slievemoughanmore, Ma, with the dog."

"Sure, they said on the news that dogs can catch it," she grumbled.

"But I haven't seen anyone but you and the ladies," I assured her. "Sure, there's no one for miles." My heart shrank in my chest. No one but the cottage ladies. As ever. Maybe I sneak down to the town and catch it.

But I couldn't do that to Ma.

I wished she'd let the dog in the house at night. He's so little, he could curl up, right here beside me, in my bed. I longed to feel a breathing body beside me and give it the love I remember I felt for Father, that I haven't felt since. Like when he came home from work, with the black dust all over his face. The dust that was like black flour and that finally took Father away from us.

I pulled the quilt up over my head and turned my back to the door. Ma was noisy in the kitchen, as she always was. I heard every scuff of the chair on the tiles and the splosh of the water as she washed her teacup in the basin that had lived in the sink since the days of Father.

Ma stood at the doorway for a moment. I held my breath. She took a step back into the kitchen, turned out the light, then shuffled back into the bedroom. It took her several minutes to take her clothes off and an age to put on her nightie. She grunted and sighed as she finally lay down. She was getting slower.

I wished our beds were further apart. At this distance, if I had it and coughed, she'd catch it. I pictured the room, hidden in the ink of the dark, and mapped out a better layout. My bed in the far corner and hers by the door, nearest the kitchen, since she was always last to bed. We could move her sewing bench into the centre, like a divider, then surely, her noises would be muffled by the rolls of fabric. I'd not have to hear her farts in the night; that pffft sound that made me uneasy, or the wet chewing sound she made every night. I wanted to suggest it – I had for years – but I feared her face would cloud over red and I'd be sent outside in the cold, with the dog.

Then, when she finally let me in, her silence would fume at me and stop me from eating, like when I asked to have my own bath water, just fresh for me, not after hers.

I'll say it tomorrow. I'll be afraid no more. Father would want me to. Surely a man of 50 can ask his Ma to move the beds into a better layout? Surely, it was my time – to say what *I* wanted?

The dog cried in the night, outside my window.

I hoped he didn't catch it, and die – before I did.

Lesley Walsh is currently writing a trilogy for children and a novel of contemporary fiction. A graduate of the Seamus Heaney Centre, QUB, one of her stories written for the course was runner-up in an international competition. The following short story is inspired by true events.

Autumn by The Shore
Mairead Breen

(where the Mountains of Mourne sweep down to the sea)

This early October day
could have fooled us into
thinking it was May.

This sun, dazzling over Donard,
warms walkers, gawkers, talkers,
who've journeyed coastward

to taste the tangy sea breeze
on the meandering promenade,
by pampas grass and yucca trees.

Mairead Breen is a native of Co Armagh, Mairead settled in South
Down, near picturesque Warrenpoint, over thirty years ago and loves
her adopted county. She teaches young people with special needs and
is a proud grandmother of four. She began writing poetry relatively
recently and also writes short stories and flash fiction.

Song on the Shore
Florence Heyhoe

On the beach between Warrenpoint and Rostrevor, a lone woman meanders, grey pebbles shifting under her feet. The tide, half way out, ripples along the border between Cooley and Mourne in Carlingford Lough. Seagulls drop mussels as they swoop by, Oystercatchers stab at the sand, and waders wash and drink in the river, where it gurgles across smooth stones towards the grey expanse of mudflats. Above the woman stretches a blue sky, rippled with white clouds like sand at low tide.

Rocks like giants' heads lie covered by green algae helmets, tendrils of seaweed drying in the sun. The woman stoops, collecting handfuls of shells, and sings *Molly Malone*.

Yellowed limpets lie, pierced, where they've been stabbed by beaks or smashed against rocks. Periwinkles lie in hollows in the sand, scarred and scraped by the tides. Tower shells curl like cream horns among the barnacled stones, and the giants' fingers of razor shells. Blue and green sea glass, smooth as porcelain, scatters the sun's rays into sprinkles of light.

Sea and moon push and pull in their infinite tug-of-war, churning and rolling these jewels of the sea, grinding them into particles of sand that whisper stories from the past.

Standing within a stone circle on the shore, her arms outstretched, the woman turns to stare through time and into the beyond.

She sings a song of breaking waves, accompanied by war cries of invading Vikings, by marauding giants, smugglers, storms and wrecks.

The medley flows out to fill the space between the North and South, between sea and sky, filled with both gratitude and lament.

Florence Heyhoe lives in Warrenpoint, Co. Down. She writes both poetry and prose inspired by her observations of life and the natural world. Her work appears in various books, including *CAP anthologies*, *Her Other Language* and *The Trees of Kilbroney Park*.

Scenting Change at Mount Stewart
Karen Mooney

A fresh breath within these walls.
Inhaled through acceptance, exhaled to still dissent,
cool heated contentions, making room for change.
Halls of history, position, privilege, furnished
with persuasion. Where righteous truths
are laid bare by the season, dressed with poise
and traded as views to harness the heart.

Elements converse here.
A microclimate within which many facets
of diverse natures are gathered to relax,
resolve, reconcile. To propagate new outlooks
with kernels of understanding.
Sought out, stripped of position, retitled, plied
with enchanting views to transform the horizon.
Herbaceous borders were created in this fashion too.

Effecting change, then and now,
through a legion of volunteers,
making a mark, a difference, shifting borders of mind,
providing sanctuary from and for the winds of change.

A calm oasis, secure from the lough's ebb and flow.
Yet, reflecting the migratory nature of life
of a custodian who recognised the whispering scent
of change in a desolate political grassland.

This poem was written in memory of Edith, Lady Londonderry, founder of the Women's Legion, for her prominent role and how she used her house and gardens.

Subtle reference is made to her favourite perfume, Elizabeth Arden's Blue Grass, a bottle of which is displayed among the Trust's collection at Mount Stewart.

Karen Mooney has been scribbling lyrics and poetry and since 2016. Her work has been published in USA, UK and Ireland. Most recent publications include *Fevers of the Mind, Re-Side Zine* and Poetry NI's *Four x Four*. She will be releasing a pamphlet with Hedgehog Poetry Press this year.

Home Truths
Kelly Creighton

Side-streets are where the secrets are kept,
even now, next town down, I rarely return.
Reluctant migrant when my adopted town is lacking
something – a hairdresser I trust,
who I have used for twenty years,
where, for the first time, I am recognised
on the conveyor belt.
It is the anonymity I like here in my old town;
familiar faces who need not call you out
or say hello; like a home full
of people, home from work or school.

stop the bus I need a wee wee
a wee wee bag of chips – and a banana

It *was* a lovely day the day we went to Bangor,
cutting into car parks where memories live
in this town of rich and poor and little between,
the young and the old – I am
in between this town and one of past,
of marriage, youth and reversing back…
everywhere we go-oh!
they shouted on the school bus

people always ask us, who we are
and where do we come from
and we tell them
we're from Bangor.
Bonny, bonny, bonny, bonny,
bonny, bonny Bangor

swiping receipts from the cold dead lips
of ATMs and filling your pockets,
your mother will find them and believe
for a small time that you have secret stashes
in every building society in town,
there is talk of them sorting out the seafront
there is still talk of them sorting out the seafront,
pictures form in your mind of Spanish towns,
children ten pin bowling and behaving.
They should have Bangor
like this – something for everyone…

and if they can't hear us
we shout a little louder

it would keep the children busy, keep them
out of trouble, off the streets

Bonny, bonny, bonny, bonny Bangor

Kelly Creighton lives in Co. Down and facilitates creative writing classes for community groups and schools. She curated *The Incubator* literary journal for five years. Her books include *The Bones of It*, *Bank Holiday Hurricane* and *The Sleeping Season*. *Problems with Girls* will be released in November 2020.

Homecoming
Rosemary Tumilty

I stand today, as a woman, in the place that changed my life: the place I call home.

Tiny dots on the horizon. An ominous, angry evening sky. Waves chewing at the outer pier and harbour walls. The hood of my raincoat flapping wildly as a seagull beating against storm clouds seeking shelter; my ears partly exposed and freezing. Others, sheltering in cars, eyes cast to the horizon. Hope and anxiety palpable in the air. A grey seascape tattooed on my brain, as slowly, imperceptibly, the dots glow brighter, moving from the horizon onto the grey matted blanket that undulates and threatens to envelop them, like Jonah swallowed whole, floating in the belly of a whale, leaving not a trace.

And I remember.

The overwhelming tang of herring, seaweed, and diesel oil claw at the back of my throat. I am wrapped in my dad's oversized jumper, the sleeves rolled up time and again on my childish arms, but there is nowhere on the planet I'd rather be on a damp, windy August evening.

I jump down from the harbour wall, little bare-toed, summer-sandaled feet splash through miniature veins of river tributaries on the rough concrete of the pier, then scurry after

Dad's size-12 footsteps. Little fingertips run along the high harbour wall; the early evening harbour lights catch the ripple motion as each of his footprints fade away.

One by one boats chug past us as we stand, hand in hand, watching as they navigate the tight twists and turns of the inner harbour walls, past the ice-house and green-mossed slipways, leaving the angry sea and its hungry belly behind for another day.

Taking their berths, we stand alongside on the quay among ropes thick as my wrists, as crates of fish are thrown from the deck of the small skiffs, up into the strong waiting arms of the crew, glistening arcs of salt and fish scales trailing in their wake. The crew's features are softened now that feet are rooted on concrete. Crates are stacked before being loaded onto trollies, the boats swaying and dipping as voices call instructions from below deck, and shout jovial obscenities. The catch, boat, and crew all now safe in the harbour's embrace, the day though not yet over for these weary hard-working men.

We shout down to the crew, "Any chance of a few herring?"

They laugh and shout for a bag.

Wafts of diesel, the heaving of grimy yellow and orange oil-skin-clad fishermen; boats jockeying and grinding for position against the harbour walls; reels and monstrous ropes heaved ashore; heavy dulcet tones ringing out among barely broken voices; the clatter of plastic crates and the torrential outpouring of ice; machinery and winches whining in the evening air; drizzly rain clinging to jackets, jumper and hair; chains and nets for repair, clanking, grating, catching: a cacophony of vibrant harbour noises, sights and aromas absorbed by a young mind.

Suddenly, from somewhere, a plastic bag materializes, and six or eight weighty beauties are slipped into their travel bag and carried as precious cargo back to the car after much waving, smiling and the offering and refusal of money; the bag dripping and awash with fish oils.

A peek into the bag on the way home and I know at a glance there'll be plenty of roe on the pan this evening; these beauties will deliver. I'll help my mum and granny with the washing, gutting and cleaning, dipping the fish and roe into flour then listen to the sizzle and skite from the pan on the Aga, as warm smells fill the kitchen and Mum will laugh and shout for someone to open the back pantry door to let the smell out! Teeth will sink through the crispy skin into the soft sweet salty flesh; the roe, squeezed between tongue and roof of the mouth, popping with flavour, and a cut of McCann's loaf, twice the size of my hand, to accompany the offerings, swiping fish skeletons and bones about the oily plate, wiping it clean. Happy, smiling, laughing faces round the table.

Yes, a feast awaits indeed.

When I was a child on cold wintery nights in London, waiting for the summer to come so that I could go home, Kilkeel harbour would sing to me – for the draw of the sea is too great for a mere human being.

Today though, I see the grey tattoo etched on liquid sunken eyes of those who look to the horizon, waiting.

Forever waiting.

> In Kilkeel I have come home.
> With the sea I am as one.
> I am at peace.

Rosemary Tumilty, a nursery school manager, singer/songwriter, poet and playwright from Kilkeel, has won two scholarships: the Yeats International SS (2018) and the John Hewitt International SS (2019), and received an Arts Council NI SIAP Award (2019/2020). She has contributed to several anthologies including *'Embrace the Place'*, with the Armagh Rhymers.

Greyabbey
Meg McCleery

It's the rooks that draw us in, sweeping
and swooping amongst the trees:
A cacophony of noise.
I wonder what the Anglo-Norman Invader
John de Courcy thought when surveying his conquest?

I can see Affreca, his bride, as she sits
in her Abbey, sewing with her ladies at her feet,
her golden locks flowing to her lap, her
green gown stained from walking in wet grass.
A Founding Invader, at home in this cold climate.

I wonder what the Gaelic Brian O'Neill thought,
when protecting the Abbey from the English Invaders,
he watched the flames rise high in the night
destroying that which he was saving?

Fast forward to Montgomery, Anglo-Scot Invader,
making restoration, and his immortal mark.
Now long established.
Claiming his place in history.

Out in the graveyard, as the sun glints through
the Abbey, casting shadows on those ancient stones,
a history is there for the reading.
Rebellions quashed, United Irishmen lie sleeping.
And on a still night, when the rooks have gone to nest,
You can hear the disquiet amongst the silence.

Meg McCleery is a retired college lecturer from Belfast now living in North Down. She taught literature and creative writing at college and in Community Arts and Women's Centres. Recently she won third place in the Annual Bangor Poetry Competition in 2019. She is now working on her first novel.

Marian Café
Paula Ryder

Although we slept in our house on the 'back road' (Station Road) in Crossgar, we lived in Marian Café, on the 'front street' (Downpatrick Street). As a child of the Fifties and Sixties, our Rodgers' family chip shop always seemed busy. My mother, Margaret, had no official business hours – just worked hard from early morning 'til late at night. Occasionally, she'd invite the last, lingering customers across the path to Marian House, for a wee sing-song around the piano. I'd slip down from bed, sit on the bottom stair and listen.

All meals were eaten in the shop. I deliberately sat at the table beneath a redundant hatch window that had been sealed with a cardboard hoarding, advertising Capstan cigarettes. Well… it was almost sealed. It had an inch-deep vertical gap. I now confess to squeezing many spoonfuls of unwanted vegetables – on numerous occasions – behind said advert. I didn't ever think about the disgusting, decaying food mess, and I never once noticed a bad smell!

On cold days, locals would shop, then stay on a while and huddle by the open fire to hear or relay the latest gossip. I did my schoolwork at the nearest table to the blazing fire. Sometimes, I'd sit right in front of it, chair tilted back, feet planted high on the tiled fireplace wall, trying to warm my chubby thighs (no trousers for little girls then) watching as I became redder-legged with each tale's telling.

Above my study table, sellotaped to the wall, was a long, coloured poster for our 'Festival' cinema's monthly fare, with a new film every two days. I immediately recall the whimsical *Darby O'Gill and the Little People*.

Thrilling stories, exotic locations and now-legendary film stars, all appeared right there, on the big, mesmerising Silver Screen before us. We devoured everything: from 'B'-rated monster movies and sci-fi, through westerns and war films, to joyous musicals and romantic classics. Hollywood was for epics, Elstree for comedy. Our wee picture-house up the lane – with its tatty velvet seats, ice-cream lady and countless hours of glorious escapism – still fills me with nostalgia. How I wish I had even one of those posters as a memento. Magical memories!

What made our shop so special was not the perfectly-fried fish 'n' chips, or the hearty bowls of thick, flavoursome broth on a cold day, or even the cooling ice-cream pokes, sliders and sundaes for Belfast folk on their way to Tyrella Beach in the summer. It was because it was the *in* place to go if you were a teenager or in your early twenties. We had a *jukebox*!

This beautiful, bellowing beast sat in our 'top shop' (adjoined to the main 'bottom shop'), with its five double-sided panels of recording artists' names and, more importantly, a full-width, rib-cage row of vinyl 45's, all lined up, longing to be chosen and released in exchange for sixpence, or a shilling-for-three. Chink – money dropping; Swish – slide along to chosen record position; Clunk – selection arm lifting record unto turntable; Click – playing arm with needle activated. MUSIC! These aural rhythms just added to the excitement.

An energetic, highly hormonal collection of youthful boys and girls listened eagerly for their favourite tracks. Not for them the 'square' story-songs like *Tom Dooley,* or catchy numbers from Perry Como or, even worse, the homely tones of Caledonia's Andy Stewart, with his wee twinkly eyes and the lilting kilt, singing *Scottish Soldier.* No! What really got the place buzzing was… good old Rock 'n' Roll!

Many a wee romance blossomed for the youngsters hanging around our jukebox, listening to the energy of Chuck Berry, Joe Brown and Marty Wilde or playing Connie Francis ballads about cheatin' love and broken hearts.

The music played in our shop really connected with the local youth. Idols like Bobby Vee and Adam Faith (on whom I had a massive crush) sang about fancying someone… or sweet dreams… or teenage angst. I really loved the soulful, mellow tones of The Drifters, and Sam Cooke, and the so-exciting harmonies of girl-groups like The Ronettes.

This music was the heartbeat of our day, and each day was different. My mammy loved the jukebox so much that she bought and played the sheet music for much of what she heard during working hours. I can still see, in my mind's eye, the cover picture for Fats Domino's *Blueberry Hill.*

An added bonus for being family in the shop was that I didn't have to pay for any of the Plays. If it was quiet, we just opened the machine, flicked our selection switches and there it was: music on tap. Fantastic! Of course, we wouldn't do this if other people were around. The younger clientele needed to use their own choice of record as bait for luring the opposite sex!

The local girls copied the look of their favourite female stars, wearing flicked bouffant, beehive or short demi-perm hairstyles, usually created by Mrs Madine in the hairdressing salon across the street. Hairbands (we sold a variety of them) were optional.

Dresses with tight waists and full skirts were popular, sometimes with added double-layer petticoats for the weekend dances, worn with strappy, kitten-heeled shoes or little flattie pumps.

The local guys however, didn't expend much money or effort, even for weekends. They invariably wore drainpipe jeans with turned-up bottoms, a white t-shirt and maybe a James Dean-style biker jacket or top-of-a-suit jacket.

However… they *did* wear pointy winklepicker shoes or 'brothel-creepers' and, most importantly, they had big quiffed hair-dos. What creations *they* were!

Greased back, and up, with Brylcreem and arranged to roll inwards towards the middle of the head, sitting at maybe four or five inches high and with a cheeky little quiff of hair allowed to fall forward onto the mid brow – they were genuine works of art.

The hair would be checked frequently in our glass display cases, and any fallen lock deftly put back into place with the essential, ever-ready pocket comb (another one of the many items we sold).

'Right! That's the D.A. okay again!' the Peacock would say. His pals would laugh.

Of course, in those days, I didn't know that D.A. stood for Duck's Arse and not District Attorney (I picked that up from watching *Perry Mason)*.

Sometimes the fellas and girls – especially if they fancied each other – would practice dancing together, though no smooching was allowed. Jiving routines were worked out, girls with ponytails a-swishin', guys pulling their jacket collars up, couples looking like something out of Cliff Richard's *Expresso*

Bongo. Which leads me to another memory.

In our café, there was an unspoken rule that you were either an Elvis fan or a Cliff fan – you could not, under any circumstance, be both. Allegiances were, I'd say, about 65% to 35% in favour of The King.

Certainly in our establishment, Presley ruled the roost, and his numerous singles were played on our jukebox over many years. I think I had a notion of him even before I knew what 'notions' were.

Music played another role in our Café life. In the heady days of the Showband Era, lovers of rock 'n' roll all through Ireland would dance to live renditions of the latest Hit Parade favourites. Bands zig-zagged across the country, playing in small halls for little money. The love of music and the hope of 'making it big' kept them going.

We had two dance halls in Crossgar: the War Memorial Hall and St Joseph's Parish Hall. The inventory of musicians who performed in these venues included *The Freshmen* (all the way from Ballymena) *The Carlton*, *The Gaylords* and *The Hilton*. Most of them visited Marian Café.

The bands would come to us for a meal before their gigs. Tables from the top shop would be pushed together, and the boys – and frequently a girl for front-of-band vocals – would sit down to generous fish suppers with peas and platefuls of bread and butter and the biggest pots of tea. They'd play the jukebox, chatter loudly, wolf down their food, and away!

Our reward was not only the extra income but, more importantly, a postcard of the band, doubly impressive if it was autographed. We had a fantastic collection of these cards on display, pinned around the shelf that held Gallagher's various-strength cigarettes, Senior Service, Woodbine, Park Drive and tins of 'baccy' for the pipe-smokers.

Memories of Marian Café flood my mind: mammy making batter for a first fry of fresh fish from Ardglass, after she had filleted it with her long-bladed 'gully' knife; Cantrell & Cochrane's lemonade in a wealth of flavours; gigantic stainless steel tubs of ice cream, two flavours only – vanilla or raspberry ripple; Smith's crisps with the wee blue bag of salt included; flat-pack chewing gum with Football Cards or Flags of the World Cards; white and green *Avery* scales for weighing out a quarter of whatever, chosen from the long line of glass Sweetie Jars; the long 'bottom-shop' counter with its row of diner-style stools.

Marian Café was small but mighty, built on hard work and dedication. It was a cross-community venture before its time, a sociable place for young and old alike, a hub of humour, fun and wonderful, exciting music. It sustained our family for nearly twenty years and paid for our education.

Even now, over sixty years on, I find modern-day chip-shops wanting. My mammy (and daddy – by day a *Man-from-the Pru* Insurance agent) fried the nicest fish and chips I've ever tasted. Marian Café was The Tops!

I dedicate these memories to my parents – Margaret and Hugh Rodgers – and to Minnie and Mother Murray of Brookvale, Downpatrick Street, Crossgar.

Paula Ryder from Crossgar and Antrim, writes 'every-day life' poetry – political, humorous and nostalgic. She enjoys writing classes and reading at cultural events and festivals. Her most recent publications include *Multiple Wounds*, in the *Of Mouth 2020 Anthology 'Her Other Language'*, in support of Women's Aid.

County Fermanagh

*The talent in County Fermanagh never lets us down. We open this chapter with a poem by **Trish Bennett**, followed by a wonderfully twisty story from the pen of **Cinnomen McGuigan**.*

* **Trish Bennett** brings us a second poem, Sweet Spot, then **Jennifer Brien** tells a story of the changes in a house she grew up in, and the way it adapted to the needs of the family. This chapter is brought to a close by **Jenny Methven**, with her gentle observations of life on a country lane.*

Raucous of Wings
Trish Bennett[i]

When you live in the sticks,
you'd think there'd be peace.

Not a hope this week
with the racket of winged things.

House Martins crowd telephone lines,
swoop down in a chitter-chatter.

A village of starlings lands in the cherry tree.
Their raucous upsets the tits enough

to flit their feeder
and return to defend their perches.

The Catalina's returned
to do laps of the lough,

bringing back the sounds of the '40s.
She takes the turn so low,

her engines throom-throom over our home.
She looks like she'll belly-slap Lunney's hill,

but no,
she glides on to land at St. Angelos.

When she vrooms over the room
on the umpteenth turn,

I imagine our lane,
a rough track then,

fit only for horse and cart,
and hardy folk.

The noise of herself
and her Sunderland friends

flying low to land
on their Atlantic return.

As they roar over stone-walled homes,
women grab the beads and bless themselves,

when their sacred hearts
are rattled.

Trish Bennett is a Leitrim writer and performer who's settled herself into a bee-loud glade in Fermanagh. She's won or been placed in over a dozen competitions. In 2019, the Arts Council of Northern Ireland awarded her a SIAP grant to aid the development of her debut poetry collection.

Do They Ever Really Change?
Cinnomen McGuigan

"Thanks for welcoming me to the group. I'm Niamh, 37, washed up, tired out, as you can see." I swallow past a lump in my throat. "He came into my life just over three years ago."

I'm met with a chorus of "Welcome Niamh," and looking out at all the smiling, exhausted faces, I know I can tell my full truth here. These women look as if they've been through the toxic-relationship mill too. I've searched hard to find a safe place to vent my domestic frustrations, and I'm excited to think that the Minor Hall at the Bawnacre Centre might just be it.

I take a deep breath, a swig of cold tea, and begin my testimony.

"I know I don't need to say this, but I want to start by telling you all that I love him without question. More than life, more than air; he just completes me. And he's so gorgeous. I mean stunningly beautiful: eyelashes to die for, so much so that he turns heads everywhere we go. Anyone who meets him, loves him. I might as well be invisible, when we're together." I see smiling faces around the room encouraging me, and nods of agreement from those that know us.

"He can actually be really sweet and loving, and at those times, he makes me feel like the best person alive. I can spend

159

hours, just watching him. I stare at him as he sleeps, and I'm still entranced. He captivates me. But there is a downside."

The nods become more emphatic, there's the odd murmur of recognition, and I know that they get it.

"He is literally the laziest person I know. Everything at home is on me. I do all the cooking and cleaning, whilst hanging on by the skin of my teeth to my day job – I'm a writer, when I get a minute – while he does nothing but bring a pile of mess and demands. He always wants something, and no matter how tired I am, he just doesn't seem to care. It's all hands on deck if he needs a drink, or food, or a bath, whereas I get nothing. What if *I* want to eat? Well, I know where the kitchen is. I want a drink? Sure, isn't the fridge right there? A bath? Wow, that is the height of luxury that I just don't have time for anymore. Even a quick shower before bed is more than I can hope for these days."

I take another deep breath as I scan the room.

"But he's so lovely and charming, and he has a smile that makes me melt. He invariably wakes in a good mood and is still smiling at bedtime, when I'm a mad wreck. Sure, when he gets upset, he can be a monster. I mean, he's not violent or anything, but his tone and volume is enough to make me shake. And he sometimes throws things."

I register the shock on a few faces and dial it back a little.

"Nothing of mine, thank God, only his own things – but it is still scary, when he gets that wound up. There's just no talking to him when he's in a rage. And then, when he calms down, it's like I dreamed it would be. I want to talk about it, to make it right, but he just wants to kiss and cuddle as if it never happened. Working out what's going to tip him over the edge is a guessing game. His communication skills are definitely lacking. I really wish he could tell me exactly what is wrong, how I can fix it, or what can be done to make sure he doesn't get upset like that again. But he doesn't; in fact I don't think he can. And so we both get more and more frustrated; him getting more crabby, and me waiting for the other shoe to drop. It's a no-win situation."

The nods show the group is back on side, so I reach for a Rich Tea biscuit and carry on.

"But, for me, the final straw, what's making me crazy right now, is that he wants constant attention and doesn't appreciate anything that I do. It's so bad that he will drop food and not bother to pick it up, or even tell me it's there, so I inevitably find it by walking through something gross. Or, worse, I notice a dead smell coming from under the sofa. And he always wants me to accommodate his plans. I'm at his beck and call 24-hours a day. So, we invariably do what he wants, when he wants it, regardless of what I had planned. If he wants to eat, then its dinner time and everything gets put on hold till we eat. Yeah, you heard me right, I said till *we* eat, cos if he's hungry, then I'm eating. He'll even try to force food into my mouth, so it's just easier to share meals with him."

The mumble of agreement counters the odd eye-roll from the assembled women, but I'm relieved I can finally say all this out loud.

"He wants to be the centre of my world. He expects literally all of my attention. I have to be laser-focussed on him at all times. Even when I've spent all day with him, he wants more. I'm on call night and day to make him happy. There are times I can't wash, or cook, or sleep, because he needs me to be there for some imaginary thing. That's why I'm tired, well a bit that and a bit that I find myself sneaking out of bed in the early hours to get on top of my normal chores, like unloading the dishwasher and doing laundry. Heaven help me if I want to get some work in – that is borderline impossible right now. This month, he's even muscled in on those few snatched moments I *do* manage, by waking me in the middle of the night for something or other, with no regard to how knackered I'll be the next day. I love to hang out with him, and I know he's having sleep issues, but I need my sleep, too. I care about how this all affects me and our relationship, whereas he doesn't."

I grimace as I take one more swig of my cold tea.

"I'm starting to wonder if the heart-melting smiles and the wonderful snuggles make up for all the downsides. They used to, but now it is getting worse, and he's getting more demanding. I'm finding myself starting to reassess if it's all worth it. Maybe it's time to get some help, and that's why I'm here today. Like I said at the start, I love him more than breathing. But some days, it just feels like it's too much. I've spoken to family and friends, and even my husband, but they just make excuses for his behaviour. It's all, 'Niamh, he's three. He's just a toddler. It'll get easier', but I don't get it. He's my first kid so I don't really know. Do they ever really change, or is he just toxic?"

Though the crowd had bristled slightly at various moments as I recounted my story, the groans and the chorus of "Toxic, defo!" and "Kids, why do we have them?", followed by raucous laughter made me feel that I was right: the Irvinestown Bad Mothers' Baby Club was where I had found my tribe.

Cinnomen McGuigan completed her third degree recently, and it was at the Open University that she made the connections that led her to Women Aloud NI, where she is the current secretary. She fell in love with Fermanagh at first sight and has made her home here since 2011.

Sweet Spot
Trish Bennett

Lower Lough Erne viewed from Claragh Road, Blaney[ii]

Each morning,
I grasp the curtains with tired hands
and fling my arms wide.
Rings rattle in retreat on their rail
as the Fermanagh Monet fills my frame.
I await the lift like a cradled child.

Sun tackles showers on in-between days,
sprinkles of rainbow are cast upon isles.
Boats speckle the lough like white chocolate chips
rippling the mirrored reflection of sky.
My eyes soak it up as the day kicks in,
I float away on a natural high.

Each night, I take a closing fix.
Through the shadows,
Irvinestown twinkles a smile.
A handful of jewels,
draped on the end of one arm,
while I perch content on the other side.

The Stairs
Jennifer Brien

Just below the ceiling of the hall, where the edge of the stairs passes beyond the corner that supports it, there is a small triangle of nothingness. Each day, around noon, a shaft of sun from the gable window stabs through it and across the wall, like Newgrange at mid-Winter.

It was not so when my mother had the house built. Mr. Burke, who sold her the land, would not allow a full two stories, lest the windows overlook him. The loft beneath the red-tiled roof must hold only a water tank and space for lumber, and be reached by a folding ladder. For light, he allowed a window in each gable.

My mother, however, had other plans.

She had five children living with her, and her mother. There was little money left from the sale of our dead father's farm, so she employed a builder with a crooked eye. While he was building the new house, she found us a two-up, two-down terrace to rent in the village, with neither a bathroom nor a proper kitchen, and a landing only big enough to hold two doors. She and my granny slept in the front room.

Every Sunday, we would walk up the hill to see our grand new house growing. There'd be a proper kitchen, a bathroom, and a parlour that would also be a dining room. My mother would have her own bedroom and so would my granny. She'd even have a wash basin in her room! Since we were a respectable family, there'd be a separate sitting room for when the minister called. That meant there'd only be room for one more bedroom on the ground floor.

The girls would have to sleep upstairs.

My mother consulted the plans again. If the roof were just a fraction steeper, then the water tank could be squeezed under the purlin and into the eaves, and that would free up space for a north-facing room. Suddenly, the house seemed bigger. Even though it would mean going through the girls' room to get to theirs, the boys could sleep upstairs as well.

The adventure of pulling the ladder up after us each night quickly became tedious. The stairs arrived in 1969, about five years after we first moved in, just as my eldest sister started Secondary School.

She was given a room of her own, with a new dormer window to the front of the house to let light in. The local handymen framed it out in two-by-fours-and panelled it with fibreboard, leaving a tiny passage under the slope of the roof, above the space where the trapdoor and ladder had been, to access the boys' room. The stairs themselves had to be pushed as far back as possible to clear the front door, so that little triangle of space appeared at the top; just one more makeshift in a house of makeshifts. It was no beauty, but it was better than the ladder.

Over the decades that followed, the house emptied, and I began to sleep downstairs, in the room where my granny had died. The dormer windows rotted and were replaced by skylights. I demolished the walls of my sister's old room, and created a study space, furnished with the dining table that was no longer needed downstairs. From the telephone socket under the stairs, a cable snaked its way up through the triangle to my dial-up modem.

It was a new millennium. I was connected, and the world was at my feet.

Over the years, my mother grew frail in both body and mind. She could no longer climb the stairs, so I abandoned my eyrie to care for her. I cleared and tidied enough to make the ground floor comfortable, while the end rooms upstairs slowly filled with junk. Attendance allowance wasn't much, but we got by.

Then she was gone, and I was alone. The world had changed. I had changed. There seemed no place for me anymore.

"You could sell up and move to town," my brother said. "If anyone wants to buy this place, it will be for the land."

But in 2013 nobody was buying, and I wasn't sure I wanted to move, so I stayed where I was. For a long time, I didn't care how I was living, and found a certain grim satisfaction with experiments in poverty, just to see what I could put up with – but there is more to life than just surviving. Someone once said, "Don't be proud of doing anything your dead Grannie can still do better. Don't hold on to all you have until the bitter end."

I sat on the stairs, and I looked at the last of those fibreboard partitions with their peeling wallpaper.

"Whoever wants the house won't want those," I thought. "I know I don't."

I broke them down and cleared them away, until the upstairs was one space again – not just as it was before, but clear from gable to gable. I could stand at the top of the stairs and see the sky in all four directions at once. It seemed good to be able to make changes, even though I was not sure why I was making them.

That's when I saw, for the first time, the sunbeam in the hall where no sunbeam should be.

With the help of friends and neighbours, I am slowly changing the rest of the house; not for the market, but for myself and for those who come to visit.

Each summer, cycling tourists come to stay the night, and I sleep upstairs again, where I can look up through the skylight at jackdaws on the chimney, or down past the stairs and into the hall.

There are many changes still to make, but that triangle of sky that is only visible at one spot, halfway down the hall – that stays.

Jenny Brien has lived all her life in and near Ballinamallard. She is a member of Fermanagh Writers and editor of the online Arts Magazine Corncrake. She writes both poems and short stories and is currently working on a novel about Judas Iscariot.

The World of The Lane
Jenny Methven

The hare stops in front of me on the lane. It had moved so quietly, I hardly noticed it at first. Now, with its nostrils quivering, ears erect, it knows I am here and turns towards me, holding me in its gaze as I stand, not wanting to move, hardly daring to breathe.

In the time I have to observe it, I make mental notes of its size, its colour, the different browns, the small amount of black on ears and head, the angle they are held – and then the eyes: round, golden, black. With the hare caught in the shadow of the hill, it is difficult to be precise. I draw it in my head, ready to transfer it to paper and pen when I get home. Photographing it helps but this is not just an animal, it is a totem, a spirit, shapeshifting through this world and on into the next.

Then just as quietly, the hare moves on, loping off across the field with long, straight strides before it turns to follow a different, less linear route into a field, across a bridge.

I have a thing about hares. If I am lucky, I will come across one on the lane, or in the fields above the lane, and when I do, I am overwhelmed by the magic.

I have found that hares can appear just when they are needed.

Hares have meaning for me. The Mad March Hare, whose

watch is broken and stuck perpetually at *time for tea* in Alice in Wonderland; the hare of Aesop's fables, outrun by the tortoise, but most of all, the hare of Celtic mythology, eyes as round and hypnotic as the moon that stares in through the window on a dark night.

They appear at times of change in the natural calendar, Easter or *Eostre*, but also in my own world.

On another occasion, a time of turmoil in my life, I was seeking answers in a mountain lane crowded with wild flowers when I met a mountain hare.

Appearing from nowhere, it stopped for a moment, taking stock of its surroundings before bounding off across the heather and into the purple-pink distance. I watched as it went, and saw it change direction, turning towards a derelict cottage that was lit up by a carpet of the white star flowers of wild garlic that surrounded it. Then it was gone again, and the world changed. A new perspective. A chance connection with another world, with the *sidh*?*

The lane at Mullycovet by my home is an old lane. In the eighteenth century, it was a busy place as carts were brought up hill by local farmers to the corn mill for the grain to be dried and ground. Now, it is empty, no longer in use. The restored water mill stands still, but the squirrels and foxes, wood mice and others have made the place their own.

The lane reaches almost from the water's edge of the lough and leads up into the low mountain behind. This is a land of ancient limestone, caves and uncertain footholds, worn away by the streams that trickle and sometimes flood down from the mountains and hills, where there is only a light covering of earth over rock. Trees tilt at drunken angles on the hillside, moving downwards over the years as the wind and rain thrust them from their loose anchors, reminding me of the tropical sea plants that I find in fossilised form as I dig in the soil, ancient relics from when this area was covered by a warm sea.

I've come to know it well, this lane. I set myself the task of looking, watching, keeping note of any changes in the natural world on this one lane for a year. Now I can't stop, and the plants and creatures that I see or don't see on any of my walks are fixed in my mind like friends. It gets you thinking, when you focus on a small area such as this, walking the same path nearly every day, usually accompanied by Rosie, the dog, and sometimes hijacked by George, the cat. My human senses are narrow. Rosie helps, her canine instincts usually attuned to the slightest movements. But there are so many levels, so many worlds beyond the narrow width of human vision and that, as much as anything else, is what fascinates me.

Winter snow brings the chance to follow the tracks of hare and fox or, less likely, squirrel and pine marten, but the magic is that it must be done early in the morning, before the pale sun has had chance to melt the prints.

Snowdrops force their way up through deep leaf litter in the old mill-house garden, close to the water, followed by lesser celandine, and then dog violets in clusters of deep purple shading towards mauve, holding on despite the rain that usually inundates them as soon as they optimistically appear.

Primroses and bluebells light the lane. By May, hawthorn blossom will breathe its heavy scent, attractive at first until it turns into a stench that even medieval people recognised as the same chemical that oozes from decomposing flesh. The hedgerows and sunken earthen lane-sides begin to grow in height and confidence, becoming lush and forest-like with cow parsley and the scent of honeysuckle.

Last year for the first time, I noticed wild orchids on the lane, and by the time summer came, wild roses had caught hold, palest pink and white, close to the old byre where solitary bees fly into the tiny gaps and crevices of crumbling cement. At times, it sounds as though the wall is inhabited with their humming. If I were to lean my head against the wall, would I capture a hundred years of knowledge?

While the lane may not have many humans, it is busy. Creatures each have different areas and paths and communities. Small holes in lichen and moss-covered walls are inhabited by a range of creatures.

Even fallen leaves aren't always what they seem. I once mistook a frog for leaves; he protested vocally when moved to the side of the lane. Some frogs are not so lucky.

Further into the lichen and moss covered trees, and close to the top of the stream as it cascades down into the woodland, is the home of a small mouse, who with glittering dark eyes in an outraged body, for one brief moment challenged a human giant when they accidentally bumped into part of his home's entrance.

Red squirrels live in the high-rise branches of ash and sycamore, just at the corner beside the mill, conveniently close to a whole section of hazel trees and bushes. A bit like living beside the corner shop, I suppose.

They are so well camouflaged that, unless Rosie is with me, it is usually only the end of a tail flashing past that I catch a glimpse of. But on one occasion, a fluffy, russet ball came hurtling towards Rosie and me as we walked. On seeing us, it performed a *Tom and Jerry* manoeuvre, then a right-angled turn off the lane to disappear into the trees.

With autumn, hazelnuts ripen, but there are no salmon in the stream to catch the hazelnut and find the knowledge. Hazelnuts litter the ground. While Rosie sniffs out the ripe ones, which she then cracks between her teeth to get at the nutmeat,

I gaze upon sloes, blackberries, and elderberries: rich colours, dark and deep like the season. Intricate spiders' webs are spun across the fields, glistening in the early morning, capturing ripe blackberries in the hedges. On a much more basic note, fox droppings lie around, strangely coloured from the rowan and blackberries the fox has eaten.

But I rail against the carelessness of those who use the lane to get to other places, those who throw their coffee cups and wrappers out. The studied indifference of the fly-tipper, who believes that the best place to leave a deep fat fryer is among the hazels, honeysuckle and elders. They do not care that here lie the well-worn, but normally secret, paths of crushed and flattened grasses, tunnelling through bracken and under hazel catkins that hang from dark branches over the mill stream.

And in these uncertain times, there is something comforting about the cyclical rhythm of the natural world, rather than the linear madness of humans, hurtling forward towards an unknown destination. Under a deep blue sky, the human world is quieter than it has been in a very long time.

In the field by the lane, there are two magpies. After reciting the usual greeting of, "Good day, sir. How's your family?" and spitting seven times, I will follow George the cat to the sunniest spot I can find, and begin a drawing, and remember that there were two magpies: two for joy.

Sídh, Irish folklore, a hill or mound under which fairies live. The race of fairies.

Jenny Methven lives close to the border in Fermanagh. She has had poetry published in both online and print journals. Jenny's poetry collection, *'Dancing in puddles with the Cailleach,'* is a combination of her poetry and artwork. She also writes a blog about the lane she lives on, at www.jennymethven.com.

County Tyrone

The women of Tyrone can tell a quare tale too. Renowned storyteller, **Liz Weir**, *is first, with a folktale inspired by the oral tradition of her dear, late friend, Harry Scott. Then* **Angela Graham** *gives a poem set in North Antrim, but reminiscing about a life lived in Gortin, County Tyrone after the Boer War.*

Kendra Reynolds *brings the past to life with her poem, Tulach Óg, followed by* **Aine MacAodha**, *who devotes her poetic odes to the lush lands of the county she calls home.* **Ellie Rose McKee** *harks back to darker days, as passed down by her mother.*

Aine MacAodha *brings us a second poem, Treehouse at Sloughen Glen then finally,* **Anne Murray** *rounds up this wonderful anthology with her story, Night of Stars – 1929, which tells of her family's history in Tyrone and beyond.*

The Boy with Knowledge
Liz Weir

Long, long ago in Ireland, young men and women would have to go off seeking work at hiring fairs. Twice a year labourers or servant girls would stand in line like cattle, waiting to be chosen. If hired, they had to stay for a full six months with their new master. They got no money at all if they broke their contract.

One young lad who completed his service was making his long journey back home, to a townland called Altenagh, in County Tyrone. It was a rainy night, and a chill was seeping into his bones. He thought to himself, "If only I could get a bed for the night, I wouldn't mind working for another day." He saw the lights of a farmhouse, and started up the lane to seek a dry place to sleep in exchange for his labour. As he approached the house, he met another young lad coming towards him.

"Don't go near that house!" warned the other boy. "There's a wicked, bad-tempered woman living in that house."

Our hired lad took the other young man's advice and turned back. But instead of leaving, he looked over and saw the hay shed. He thought to himself that he might spend a warm and comfortable night there. As he settled down into the straw, he had a good view into the kitchen of the farm-house. There, he noticed a good-looking young woman embracing a handsome young man.

Hungry as he was, the lad was more interested in the plate he could see on the table, piled high with tasty-looking meat. Beside it was an apple tart, and there was even a bottle of whis-key. The young man was drooling with hunger. As we say here, "his stomach thought his throat was cut!"

Just then, he heard the sound of a horse and cart coming up the gravel lane. It was soon apparent that the pair in the kitchen heard it too. The young woman's hands flew to her face, and she grabbed the handsome man and pushed him into a big barrel resting beside the fire. She then draped a blanket over it.

The hired boy watched as she concealed the plate of meat on top of a dresser, hid the bottle of whiskey behind the cur-tain, and set the apple pie at the back of the sofa. He was intrigued. He heard her open the door and say, "Oh John, you're back! I didn't think you'd make it home tonight."

"I got no decent price for the pigs, so I just came on back," was the reply.

It was none other than her husband, home unexpectedly.

Now, the lad in the hayshed was clever. He was well able to put two and two together, and he saw his chance to get a bed for the night, now that the master of the house was home. He left the hayshed and went and knocked on the door. The farmer opened it. When the lad explained his situation, the farmer took pity on him and brought him into the warm kitchen. It was agreed that he could have a night's lodgings in return for a day's work. The young wife was just serving up a simple supper of potatoes and buttermilk, so the boy was in-vited to join them. The hired lad knew that the way to a farmer's heart was to compliment him on his potatoes.

"These are great potatoes, just like wee balls of flour," he said. "They'd go great with a bit of meat."

"There's no meat in this house," the farmer replied. "I'm sorry to say."

The boy saw his chance, "Maybe I can help you there?" he said. "I'm from a place called Altenagh, and we have great knowledge; sometimes we only have to think of a thing and we can just magic it up. Let me have a go."

The boy closed his eyes, and to the farmer and his wife's surprise, he said, "Try on the top of that dresser."

The farmer walked over and of course, found the plate of meat. The wife looked shocked.

"That's amazing!" said the farmer.

"We have the knowledge," announced the boy, with a big smile on his face.

When the main course had been cleared away the young man thought he would try again. "Do you know I've got a very sweet tooth," he said. "I just love home-made apple tart."

"Ah," said the farmer. "My wife, there… oh, she's away to her bed… she used to be great at baking apple cake, but she bakes very little these days."

"Let's see if I can get some for us," said the boy, knowing that the farmer's wife had gone up to bed. He again closed his eyes for a moment or two. "Now," he said. "Look behind the sofa."

The farmer was delighted to find a freshly baked apple cake.

"We have the knowledge!" laughed the boy.

The two of them started eating, and it was indeed delicious. There was still one more discovery to be made, and this was the one the boy looked forward to most!

"That's a great drop of buttermilk, but would you have anything a bit stronger in the house?"

"There's not a drop of liquor in this house," replied the farmer, "though I'd be glad of some."

"Third time lucky!" quipped the lad, and after closing his eyes briefly, said, "have a look behind the curtain."

Sure enough, the farmer found the bottle of whiskey.

"We've the knowledge," repeated the boy, and the two of them opened the bottle and started into it.

Now, one of two things generally happens when two strangers meet over a bottle of whiskey – and this time was no exception. They either fight, or, as in this case, they become the best of friends. The drunker the farmer got, the more he talked to the boy about all his problems. He told him that things were not going well between his wife and himself; she was very distant.

At once, the boy saw his chance to help, one last time. "Let me see if I can solve the problem." He closed his eyes, and with a very serious look on his face, he said, "I know what's wrong."

"What?" asked the farmer.

"The devil's in this house!"

"What?" exclaimed the farmer.

"The devil's in this house. But I can help you get rid of him. You have to do exactly as I say and follow me."

The young lad walked over to the open fire, picked up the tongs and pushed them into the hot ashes. He urged the farmer to pick up the poker and do the same. When they were both red hot, they lifted them out and the lad pulled the cover off the barrel by the fire. He poked in the tongs, urging the farmer to plunge in the poker. The man hiding in the barrel jumped out screaming like the very devil himself and ran straight out the door and down the lane.

The poor farmer was too stunned to realise what had really happened.

"Well," said the lad. "I think you won't have any more problems from now on."

The farmer was so delighted, he led the young man upstairs and showed him into the guest room. That was a lot better than the hayshed! He sank down into a big brass bed, under a warm quilt and slept more soundly than he had in six months. The next morning, he awoke to the smell of breakfast cooking downstairs. When he came downstairs, the farmer's wife set him down a huge fry with bacon, egg, sausages, soda bread and fadge – the best meal he had been served in six months.

The farmer stood up to bid him farewell, saying, "I don't know how to thank you." There seemed to be no mention of him doing any more work and the boy was glad of that. The farmer then reached deep into his pocket and produced a five-pound note. That was more than the boy had earned during his six month's hire. He said goodbye to the farmer and went off, whistling down the lane with a big smile on his face.

When he got to the foot of the lane, he heard a rustling in the bushes and was afraid for a minute. Then he noticed the farmer's wife, who stepped out holding another five-pound note in her hand. As she pressed it into the lad's hand, she said, "Thanks for not telling my husband about me!"

And the boy with the knowledge went happily on his way, back to Altenagh.

A folktale from County Tyrone adapted by Liz Weir from the storytelling of the late Harry Scott.

Liz Weir, MBE has an international reputation for storytelling, having shared her tales in prestigious venues across five continents. Her children's books include *Boom Chicka Boom*, *Here There and Everywhere* and *When Dad Was Away*. She lives near Cushendall in County Antrim and directs the Glens Storytelling Festival. www.goastories.org.

Ballycastle Granny - her husband, Thomas Graham of Gortin
Angela Graham

The bride was late,
so a cousin from America,
fresh off the plane,
had time to show a photograph
    – our grandfather;
a face we had never, ever, seen:
fair- and fine-featured
and so like the bride
we Irish cousins swayed,
giddied by time telescoping shut.

'A handsome man!' one said,
cannily implying something shared.
Indeed, in dress uniform
of the Irish Yeomanry,
he stood both disciplined and delicate
– at his hip a sword-hilt, and his helmet,
frothily plumed.

Oh, Granny, of course he took your eye.
By the time you met him
he'd had four years fighting Boers.
A be-medalled returnee,
he was finding one-street Gortin in Tyrone
too small a field after South Africa.

As you walked towards him
down a Church of Ireland aisle,
were you giddy, given all you jettisoned?
– marrying out,
adventuring, with this man.

And yet, in time, you saw to it
his seven children would ensure
that we, his children's children,
would utterly lose sight of him –
The bride's arrived!

And he has made it from the grave
you do not share with him
to his great-grand-daughter's wedding.
Her groom can't help but turn.
We see him gasp, as though
he'd never, ever, seen
such loveliness.

Joint 3rd Prize Winner, Heather Newcombe Poetry Award, 2019

Tulach Óg (Hillock of Young Warriors)
Kendra Reynolds

Derryloran church pierces pre-historic fields, framed by thick hedge trims. Factory smoke billows slowly outward towards a smudge of grey sky. I watch daisy chain crowns dance on brows, accenting green with a yolk of colour.

Perched outside of time,
bracketed between history and modernity,
birdsong is the heart of nature beating.

The path of tourist asphalt insults history, with a lie of clear-sighted simplicity. The easy climb and descent captures nothing of feuding families, complex rivalries, generations punctuated by metal swords clanging. Only a conjunction separates the Mac Lochlainns and O'Neills as tears of sorrow saturate the soils of Donaghrisk.

With sights set on supremacy,
each drop of blood spilled is
a chimera of both family and enemy.

A ring of forest chieftains bear witness in the fort, whispering to the wind as Mother Nature conducts the ceremony – each little bird an honorary bard – while I perch in the ceremonial chair – the boulder, Leac na Rí – and listen to their lyrical lament.

Songs of wisdom are expertly cast
in hopes of shattering
the violence of the past.

Kendra Reynolds recently returned to Tyrone from the US, where she teaches creative writing in poetry and contemporary literature as Fulbright Scholar-in-Residence at the University of Tulsa and Tulsa Community College, Oklahoma. Her poems are published in journals and magazines including *The Honest Ulsterman*, *The Paperclip*, and *The Bangor Literary Journal*.

Island Home
Aine MacAodha

I've travelled very little from this island home.
My native land grounds me, keeps me in contact
with the rhythms of nature, the sound of the winds,
the call of the wild birds and the dialects of its people.

Tyrone's inland landscape of moss clad hills and flat bogs
break every now and then like an ocean wave.
Small towns and villages emerge lively and loud against the
woven landscape

One can drive for miles across back roads criss-crossing
town lands
whose names mean stony path, fairly coloured field or hill
of midges
before a village appears out of the hedgerows.

Fintona, Seskinore, over the mountain to Fivemiletown
across the side road to Sixmilecross, Carrickmore, Gortin
and to Omagh again; the view always lifts the spirit.

Gortin village is one such place, hidden within the protective
fauna
of the forest and rough mossy hills flanking the road into the
village.
Fiddle music sails up from the music store.

I may not have travelled far but this island home
where the ancestors have left their marks on the land,
in the form of art and awkward names; this will take me far
away.
in my mind at times.

Aine MacAodha boasts three published volumes of poetry, *Where the Three Rivers Meet, Muscált* and *Landscape of Self*. Her work has appeared in *Four X Four, Don't Be Afraid: An Anthology to Seamus Heaney; Doghouse Anthology of Irish Haiku; Poethead Blog, North West Words*, with some work also translated into Italian and Turkish.

Childhood Troubles
Ellie Rose McKee

Maude was playing with her dolls on the dirt floor when she heard her father come in the back. Jumping up to go and greet him, she was stopped in her tracks – hand halfway to the door handle – when she heard him whisper something. To her mother, she assumed.

Drawing back her hand, she hesitated, knowing she shouldn't listen, knowing she'd be scolded if she were caught, but unable to pull herself away. Silently, she stood, not going nearer and not backing away, locked in a stalemate with herself.

"They're going up the road," she heard her father say.

Her mother made an indignant noise. "Again?"

He didn't answer, but Maude imagined him nodding. The kitchen fell silent again and she finally pulled herself away, to the window. The little farmhouse was back from the road but still within sight of it, if you strained your eyes.

Straining as much as she possibly could, Maude let out a frustrated huff. It was only trucks she saw out there. Hardly anything worth talking about.

"What are you doing, Maudie?"

She spun around and slapped her tiny palm down on her father's bare forearm.

187

"You shouldn't sneak up on people!" she scolded, using the most authoritative voice she could muster, but he only laughed which left her no choice but to stop frowning and look up at him with a wide, toothy smile.

Then, remembering, she glanced back to the window. The trucks were gone.

"Who–?" she began to ask.

"The army," he said.

"Huh." She turned around again to sit on the sofa properly, feet dangling over the edge, wanting to ask if the army were goodies or baddies but resisting the urge.

"Daddy?" she began, instead.

"Yes, dear?"

"Will I understand things, when I'm older?"

He sighed a little and took a seat beside her. "The older I get, the less I understand."

This didn't satisfy her, but she didn't push it. Her mother didn't like how many things she asked about, but her dad always tried his best, even if he didn't always know.

She'd ask him an easy one, Maude decided: "What's for dinner?"

His smile returned. "Let's investigate," he said, lifting her onto his back and carrying her to the kitchen.

A few months later, her mother gave birth to a baby boy, her second son. There were six of them living in the farmhouse, now. Her dad said he was planning to extend it, come summer, and there was talk of electricity coming to the area.

One of their neighbours came to visit when the baby, still unnamed, was just a couple of days old. Maude was watching him intently as he slept in his makeshift cot when she heard the knock. She glanced at her mother, who was sat in the rocking chair, reading.

"Aren't you going to answer it?" Maude asked, but she got no response. "Mother? Aren't you going to—"

"It's just Mrs. Mills from down the road," said her mother, cutting off the question as if her words both answered and explained it.

Maude frowned and the knocking continued. "Would you like *me* to answer it?"

Her mother grunted. "Can't ever get a minute to myself?" she muttered, making her way to the door and swinging it wide. "Ah, Mrs. Mills! What a surprise. What can I do for you?"

Maude had followed her mother into the kitchen and was stood behind her long skirts, just peeking her head out enough to see two big eyes and an even bigger mouth – wide with a smile, and no teeth to speak of – looking back at her.

"My, my," said the mouth. "Isn't this one growing up? She'll be chasing the boys 'round soon enough."

"She most certainly will not!" Mother snapped. "What do you want?"

"Oh," said Mrs. Mills, her mouth hanging even more open. "Didn't mean anything by it, I just… never mind. I brought a gift, for the babby."

Maude couldn't see her mother's face from where she stood, but she assumed her eyes narrowed at talk of presents.

"Oh?" was all she said.

"Yes," said Mrs. Mills, sounding excited as she handed over her parcel. "I hope you like it. Knitted it myself."

"It's very… thoughtful," said Mother. "I've got to get on making dinner now."

"Right you are," said Mrs. Mills, as the door closed in her face.

As soon as Mrs. Mills had disappeared back up the lane, Maude watched as her mother tossed the handmade blanket onto her rag pile, used for cleaning up spills.

"You don't like it, Mummy?" she asked, confused.

"Of course, I don't! It's an offence. Can't believe she had the nerve!"

Maude cocked her head to the side before making her way to the rag pile. "Is it–?" she began, cutting herself off and then re-starting the sentence afresh. "Is it because of the colours?"

Her mother ignored her, making her way back to the baby, so she assumed she'd got it right. Again, she was aware of a nagging feeling, deep inside her, that there was something she was missing. How a beautiful new baby's blanket, embroidered with orange, green, and white, could be so bad.

***

It was the next year that the family got their first television set. Maude's mother would never let her watch it unaccompanied, and even *with* company she had a nasty habit of standing directly in her line of view – folding laundry, or some such. That was until, one day, her mother was out shopping, and her father had fallen asleep watching the news, meaning there was no one to censor whatever it was they'd been trying to keep from her.

Footage of explosions, gunfire, and fighting filled the screen. Her eyes – wide enough to drive a tractor through – might as well have been glued to it.

"Daddy," she said quietly, before becoming louder and more insistent. "Daddy!" She heard him stir behind her but still didn't look away. "Things have gone wrong, daddy! What's happening?"

In a low, gruff voice that she'd never forget, he said, 'The Troubles.'

Making no sense of it, Maude repeated the words over to herself. It was the first time she'd heard them, but it certainly wasn't the last.

Tree House at Sloughen Glen
Aine MacAodha

On our way to Sloughen Glen, deep in the hills of Drumquin
we hardly notice the climb; yet feel it in our fume-filled lungs.
Out of the side of a hill, amid brambles and giant ferns
a shell of a house appears with postcard views out over the
Tyrone countryside.

The gift of life still grows from its un-thatched roof: a gift
in the form of a blackthorn tree. It grows with pride
up through the rooms holding, I'm sure, stories in its trunk.
Memories of a time when its hearth was lit and life flourished.

I think of the family who may have lived there
children playing in the yard, a few livestock, life.

I listen to the quiet sounds of spring and remember that
the regeneration of small towns has crept nearer and nearer
to the beauty spots. One day this may well be gone.

Perhaps great grandchildren will return one day
seeking their ancestral home. They may;
and find life grows there still.

Night of Stars 1929
Anne Murray

Oft, in the stilly night,
Ere slumber's chain has bound me,
Fond memory brings the light
Of other days around me

Thomas Moore

Mice were rustling about in my bedroom fireplace again. When it's cold, they would head indoors in their dozens, looking for a bit of warmth and maybe something to eat, for no doubt they were as half-starved as the rest of us. They wouldn't find much in our house. We'd scarcely enough for ourselves, and what we did have was expertly covered up and sealed by Mam.

Before she married my Dad in 1912, she'd been parlour maid for the Richardsons, a wealthy Quaker family in Moyallon, Co. Armagh. Annie Jane Drain, my Mam, had worked her way around the household until she knew all the jobs, especially how to shield food from mice.

Vermin infestation was commonplace, here in the depths of the Tyrone countryside where mam and dad had settled in 1919, after they'd tried emigrating to Australia and then returned home. The mice had a peculiar musky smell which was especially strong that night. It gave me the heebie-jeebies. I shivered under the bedclothes, willing the little rodents to go outside.

Johnny Leitch, my Dad, was working as a hired hand in Canada at this time, breaking in wild horses. Mam said he'd been searching for peace since his first wife, Caroline, died aged 22 during her first pregnancy. Johnny's brother, Henry, had found happiness in farming; perhaps Johnny had hoped to find it, too, by buying his own farm here in Tyrone. Only, he hadn't thought to discuss it with Mam first.

Then all our cows died, and the heart went right out of him. Dad had taken the shotgun to the barn to shoot himself, but Mam talked him down, persuading him to go to Canada for work instead. We'd all cried with relief. He'd been gone now for six months and we wouldn't see him again until he'd earned enough to bring the farm back to life after its losses.

In the meantime, the three of us would toil in the fields for long hours, and care for the remaining animals: Mam, me, aged eight, and Alec, my older brother who, at ten, was now the man of the house.

It had been 10 years since they'd come back from Australia where'd they done well, returning home with a fair few sovereigns. They had been optimistic for a new beginning back in Ireland, but all that this remote, bleak farm had done was to guarantee them both years of hard labour.

This was a life far removed from the one Mam had dreamed about, one where she could use her brains. She had a good mind and proved it by running a post office and railway station near a gold mining town in Queensland, way out in the bush, while Johnny had worked the railway as a Fettler.

Quaker philanthropy had also influenced her. She was active in the church, making her mark in the community by helping those living in abject poverty. Before leaving for Australia, they'd enjoyed running a small sweetshop in Belfast for a short while. But she'd seen so many families almost destitute, with starving, barefoot children a common sight. It made her heart sore that she could do so little to help them.

Then in 1919, a year after WW1 ended, they'd landed back in Ireland with much improved means, enough to lease a small shop and get more involved in charitable works. Annie began to make plans; the situation was even more urgent now as the Spanish Influenza was actively killing thousands in Ireland, especially in Belfast.

Then she found out that Dad had bought the farm. She would tell me how she'd cried for hours, mourning the life she'd never have, thwarted by his decision to spend all their money on a move to the country.

Now *he* was in Canada while the family toiled on the land, and she and their children were nearly as impoverished as those in Belfast she had pitied.

By the time I climbed into bed each night, I would be exhausted, and cold, too. I'd haul Dad's old overcoats onto the bed as extra covers and shut my eyes tight. I missed him. Going to bed on a high chaff mattress, after the corn had been thrashed, was one of our few luxuries. A pot lid, heated on the fire by mam, added to my comfort.

Pillows were stuffed with feathers from the farm fowls, along with soft rags. It didn't pay to be sentimental about animals – life and death was just part of everyday – but I didn't like it when the hens were killed, and had been shocked by one running around the farmyard, headless. After that, I'd take myself away to the top field when I saw the axe coming out.

Our bedsheets had once been flour bags but Mam bleached out the colour and words by boiling them with washing soda on a 3-legged pot on the crook, with plenty of bellows to keep them going. Mam said I was the best at the bellows, so I'd happily sit on the small stool by the fire and perform, achieving the necessary rhythmic action with pride.

Once boiled, the bags would be soaked in Sunlight for a week. Mam had learned this at Moyallon, too, as the Quakers had been linen merchants and knew all there was to know about bleaching fabrics.

One week we had a huge storm with thunderous skies, pelting rain, and flashes of lightning that went on for over an hour. Me and Ethel Graham got caught in it on our way back from Knocknaroy Public Elementary School.

We huddled by the side of the road, pressed against the big hedge that surrounded Maggie Alexander's field, and clung to each other, drenched and afraid.

It seemed a long time before Ginny Burton found us.

She was soaking wet herself when she bundled us into the horse and trap and took us to her home.

Ginny herded us through a dark, wood-panelled hall over to a roaring fire in the main room, where she fussed around us with towels and blankets. She had family from Belfast staying with her who helped, two glamorous young women in high heeled shoes. I was mesmerised. All I'd ever known were black boots that pinched so much I had to soap my heels to get them on in the morning. But there was no money for new ones.

The Burton homestead had always been a mystery to me. Now, thanks to the storm, here I was in it, along with Ethel, whose eyes were as huge as mine, taking in these new wonders: a majestic, stuffed, green Chesterfield; red and green brocade curtains with tie backs; and gold-framed pictures on the walls. We'd never seen the like.

Someone pushed a wooden fireguard aside, to allow us nearer the fire. It was collaged in postcards from faraway people and places: Australia, Canada, New Zealand. I was completely charmed by both the artistry and what it represented – a world far outside the one I inhabited, here in Mullycar, Greystone, a small farming community outside Dungannon.

But the thing that made me hold my breath with excitement was a wall of books. I was desperate to get at them, but held back for fear of seeming bold. We had few books in our house, though sometimes a neighbour would pass on a magazine called *Bright Words*, which both Mam and I would light on with joy. There was our family Bible, of course, falling apart at the seams, as Mam was a committed Christian and read it daily.

She also had old books from her childhood, such as *Uncle Tom's Cabin* and *East Lynne*. I could have recited these books backwards, but there'd never been spare money for new books.

When we left for home, I brought away with me a new, exciting ambition to read more books but I also brought a heavy heart, aching with an envy I'd never known before. I'd caught a glimpse of a world never meant for a wee girl living up a country lane like me, one who'd only ever known hardship.

When we arrived home, Mam's face was wreathed with concern until she heard how well we'd been looked after. The Burtons were kind folks.

I was soon put to work. "Sue, we need a good boil going tonight," Mam said, looking me in the eye. "For the spuds."

I kept my longings to myself, as I worked the bellows. Mam wouldn't approve of me coveting my neighbour's house, a clear breach of the Tenth Commandment. She would have seen that my head was turned, though. Nothing much got by Mam.

That evening, however, sinning was the least of my worries. I drifted into sleep, imagining a room of my own full of books and postcards, where I could read all day without having to go out into the fields.

Just as I imagined reaching up to pick a tantalising-looking book from the top shelf, something scampered across the bed-clothes. I opened my mouth to scream, but too late. With a swift patter of clawed feet, it leapt onto my lips, whipping my teeth with its tail.

At first, the trauma had me paralysed.

Then, I exploded into action, grabbed it by the tail with one hand and pulled back the clothes with the other. I leapt out of bed, holding the wriggling creature at arm's length, and managed to stumble through the pitch darkness to the farmhouse door. I flung it out into the night, as far from me as I could.

Chest heaving, sucking in cold night air that filled my lungs with ice, the magnitude of what had happened slowly dawned on me.

Dear Lord, help me: I'd nearly swallowed a mouse!

That, surely, must have been the hand of the Almighty, telling me that I needed to be careful what I coveted.

Head hung in shame, I prayed for forgiveness. Then I lifted my eyes to the heavens to appeal directly, in case he hadn't heard me the first time.

A new moon hung in a midnight sky strewn with stars. Millions of stars. A celestial feast of diamonds. This glorious vision drove all thoughts of the mouse from my head. Instead, I was stunned by the immensity of the universe and its treasures, laid out above me, like a gift.

My eyes adjusted to the darkness; there was the Plough, just as Miss Marshall had drawn it on the blackboard. And there, right there, was the North Star. And *there* was a white streak across the sky. I gasped. A Shooting Star! Surely, that was a sign from the heavens? A promise of something greater in my life. A life, perhaps, far away from poverty, without mice for bedfellows.

Miss Marshall had said that a shooting star meant you'd been chosen to make a wish, and the heavens would grant it. I closed my eyes and wished as hard as I could.

Please... please... send me a wall of books. Just a couple of hundred, and postcards. Lots of postcards.

Oh, and a pair of high heeled shoes, please.

Ireland, the land of saints and scholars, my mother always said. Well, I was no saint but surely I could be a scholar?

When I climbed back into bed, hauling Dad's heavy overcoat over my head, the familiar, safe aroma of his War Horse pipe tobacco enveloped me, warming me as I drifted back into sleep to dream once more of bookish adventures.

In her own bed, perhaps Mam was dreaming, too. Dreaming of a life where she and dad could raise their family comfortably, run a corner shop and balance the books enough to make a difference to the barefoot children of Belfast.

Dreaming of what might have been.

Anne Murray has kept diaries and journals all her life, as did her mother, Sue McMahon (nee Leitch) before her. Recently, Anne has been collating her mum's rich memories of growing up in Mullycar, Co. Tyrone into short stories. "Night of stars, 1929" is an excerpt from those memories.

Endnotes

---

[i] Raucous of Wings - Trish Bennett
Previously Published:
Epoque Press, Ezine, Issue 6, Nov. 2019.

[ii] Sweet Spot - Trish Bennett
Previously Published:
Corncrake Magazine, July 2019, online edition, Editor: Jenny Brien.
The Bee's Breakfast Anthology, 2017, Beautiful Dragons, Editor Rebecca Bilkau.

Printed in Great Britain
by Amazon